Gangsta Shyt

CATO

**Lock Down Publications
Presents
Gangsta Shyt
A Novel by *CATO***

Lock Down Publications
P.O. Box 1482
Pine Lake, Ga 30072-1482

Visit our website at **www.lockdownpublications.com**

Lock Down Publications
Like our page on Facebook: Lock Down Publications
@www.facebook.com/lockdownpublications.ldp
Cover design and layout by: Dynasty's Cover Me
Book interior design by: Shawn Walker
Edited by: Tumika Cain

Acknowledgments

I wanna thank Ca$h and Shawn Walker (Coffee) of LDP for giving me the opportunity to display my penmanship and writing skillz to the world. Thus far, throughout this entire process, from the beginning to now, they have been helpful, supportive, business-like, and on point in the release of my urban crime novel, Gangsta Shyt.

If there are any aspiring and up and coming authors out there who wish to write in urban genre, I highly recommend them.

Author Cato.

CATO

Chapter 1

Mr. Proficient

A well-dressed, jewelry wearing pimp walked out of an after-hours joint, climbed into his 2015 Maybach Vert, cranked it up and it exploded into a huge fireball. The shrapnel and impact of the blast knocked out some of the nearby storefront windows. Everyone in the after-hours joint ran outside to witness the carnage. The smell of burning wires and flesh began to permeate the air as everyone said amongst themselves in shock and horror, "That's Kansas City! That's Kansas City!"

A couple of his whores who had heard the news about their man, ran up to the crowd acting as though they were distraught. They put on a performance worthy of an Oscar, the way they carried on, but no one in the crowd bothered to console them.

One cat bluntly told them, "Well, at least y'all can keep all the money y'all made tonight." His words seemed to end their grieving. After wiping away their Crocodile tears, they both disappeared into an alley together, arm in arm as they came to the realization that he was gone and they had his money to play with.

Sitting inconspicuously across the street from the carnage was a black Cadillac Escalade with dark limo tints and customized suicide doors, occupied by two men listening to the satellite radio play the old school joint, *Ready to Die*, by Biggie Smalls, as they looked on stone-faced at the gruesome spectacle. The man in the passenger seat, wearing dark shades, pulled out a silver flask, took a long sip from its contents, chuckled, and said in a cold voice, "Shoulda took his ass back to Kansas City." His partner in the driver seat, who was chewing gum, nodded his head slightly without saying a word.

As the sirens began to blare, inching ever so close to the horrific scene, the Cadillac Escalade fired up and began creeping slowly past the shocked onlookers, and the mangled, twisted hull of metal, engulfed in flames with the smoldering corpse inside. Amidst the commotion, a young girl with long box braids standing off to herself was the only one to take notice of the sinister looking ride. The driver, a handsome green-eyed cat wearing a gangsta lid on his head, winked his eye at her, causing her mouth to fly open in surprise. It was at this point, her instincts told her he was the one who had just hit Kansas City. But whether he was in fact the culprit or not didn't matter to her. She lived in the city long enough to know to keep her mouth shut. Besides, deep down inside, she felt zero sympathy for the nigga. In fact, part of her was kinda glad it was him inside that car roasting. As the pimp's charred body and what was left of his ride, burned on, the crowd of onlookers began to swell. Three talkative broads broke away to join the young girl with the braids who was still standing off to herself.

"Hey, girl, you saw what happened?" one of the broads asked the girl with braids.

"Wanda, how the hell did I see what happened when I was in the club with y'all?" she replied, angrily. "Girl, I tell you, for someone who was born and raised in the city, you sure are country as fuck. Besides, even if I did see what happened or knew who had something to do with it, I wouldn't say shit! That nigga finally got what was coming to him."

"Damn, Sugar! You sho' is cold!" the heavyset girl replied. "I feel sorry for him, even if he was a pimp."

"Naw, Shaun. Sugar is right," the other broad, a tall Amazon-looking girl responded. "Kansas City was a foul and nasty pimp muthafucka. Girl, you must have forgot what he did to Brenda's face for shorting him ten dollars? So, I'm with Sugar on this. That bastard got exactly what he deserved."

Moments later the paramedics, fire department, and the police arrived on the scene, late as usual. One investigator, short and stocky in stature climbed out of an unmarked car with a fat cigar in the corner of his mouth. His chili stained suit was so wrinkled it looked as though he had slept in it all night.

"Alright! Did anyone see what happened?" he asked in a classic Irish accent. Everyone remained silent, only mumbling among themselves and shaking their heads as if to say, "No."

"Alright! Alright! I know! I know! Nobody saw anything, right? No one ever sees anything," he said with a half smile and a look of frustration. "A man gets barbecued in his fucking car and nobody saw shit, right? Alright! Ok!" he said with his huge hands waving in the air. *I really wouldn't give a fuck if these jungle bunnies all killed each other,* he thought to himself.

Not long after the firefighters extinguished the flames, the coroner pulled Kansas City's charred remains out of the smoldering heap of metal, placed it into a long black zip-locked bag, zipped it up, and chucked it in the back of the meat wagon. As its screeching tires sped off from the scene, the stubby investigator turned and said in a cold and sarcastic voice to the other cops, "One more nigger bites the dust, aye?" They all let out a collective chuckle.

On the other side of town in Manhattan, the black Escalade pulled into the parking lot of a café. The Escalade's occupants stepped out, casually checking out their surroundings as if their heads were on swivels, before walking inside where two white men wearing dark shades and London Fog trench coats were sitting at a table smoking and sipping on coffee.

One of the white men stood up with his hands stretched out and said in a classic Italian accent, "Tony baby, how are ya? Have a seat."

Tony walked over to the table and sat down, leaving his partner standing near the entrance. The white man who greeted him with the warm reception leaned over in Tony's ear.

"Is that thing done?" he asked in a whisper.

"Well done. The same way I like my steaks," Tony replied in a cold voice. The white man let out a loud, sinister laugh as he patted Tony on his back.

"I should have known! Mr. Proficient!" he blurted out. He then turned to his partner sitting next to him who looked totally lifeless. "This man here is the best at what he do."

The lifeless looking white man nodded his head and let out an inaudible grunt, but still no expression. The white man then slid Tony a manila envelope across the table. Before opening it, Tony casually looked around the café, which was basically empty, with the exception of a couple sitting in the far back corner. Seeing a young couple in the back were busy into themselves, Tony scanned the contents of the envelope under the table that contained two hundred crisp twenty dollar bills. After counting his blood money and making sure it was all there, he slid the package inside of his sky blue leather trench coat, stood up, shook hands with the two white men, then he and his partner strutted out of the café with a gangsta swagger.

On the way home after putting in a day's work at the office, the satellite radio played *Seen It All* by Young Jeezy. After a few minutes of silent reflection, Tony broke the silence.

"Hey, Genie, I think it's time for us to do something different?"

"Like what, T?" a half asleep Genie asked.

"Like this shit is getting old, bruh. So it's time for us to do something that's a lot more profitable with less hands-on involvement."

Genie, still not fully awake said with his eyes closed, "Less hands on involvement and more profitable, huh? That nigga, Kansas City's dead ass, we never laid a hand on him and collected twenty bands. It don't get more profitable and less hands on than that, my nigga," he said in a sarcastic tone. Tony smiled and shook his head.

"No Genie," Tony said with a slight chuckle. "What we're doing in terms of money ain't shit. There's a whole world of opportunity out there for niggas like us to take full advantage of and come up in a big way, you feel me?"

"Damn, T! Sound like you trying to square up on me. You ain't going soft on a nigga, are you?" Tony smiled.

"Genie, check dis shit out, bruh. What I'm saying is, nigga, we need to expand our minds as well as our hustle, and come up in a major way. And as far as that shit about a nigga like me going soft? Don't get shit twisted, nigga!" The two partners chuckled and gave each other some dap.

"Well, what's on your mind, T? Fill a nigga in on the specifics." Tony smiled as if he already had a master plan.

"When that time comes, bruh, you will be the first one to know."

Seconds later the Escalade pulled onto the curb in front of Genie's crib. After Genie received his cut of the blood money, he climbed out of the ride and headed into his crib as Tony sped off. After reaching his own crib, Tony pulled into his backyard which was completely concealed by an eight foot high privacy fence, hopped out and immediately changed tags on his vehicle and sprayed off the removal black paint causing the truck's color to change into midnight blue as if he performed a magic trick. Always cautious and security minded, Tony entered his crib through the back door. Once inside, with pistols drawn, he disarmed the alarm and meticulously scoured each room. Once all was clear, he deactivated the heightened alert button in his brain and began to relax.

Tony's profession called for constant vigilance and extreme caution. He learned early on in his career to never underestimate anyone or take anything for granted. Anytime he had a meeting set for a specific time, he would show up at the meeting's venue

at least an hour early. And anytime he had a meeting with someone other than his partner, Genie, he would always set the location himself at the last minute and that was if he didn't change it.
These are the some of the elements, besides his patience and
close attention to detail, that made him one of the most proficient
and prolific hitters in the business. And it was for those reasons,
his reputation was legendary in the underworld.

After finally securing his crib, exhausted and ready to wind
down and relax, Tony put on some music by Anthony Hamilton
before strolling into the bathroom and running some steaming hot
bath water. He then took his two gold-plated .45 semi-automatic
pistols out of their holsters and placed them down on the side of
the bathtub. Hamilton's song *Coming From Where I'm From*
bounced off the walls of his crib. Once the tub was filled, Tony
undressed and slowly slid down into the hot, relaxing bubble
bath. Not long afterwards, he drifted off into a deep, dark sleep.

Chapter 2

Tony's Prophetic Dream

Lying in stealth on the rooftop of a building with a Remington 700 high-powered rifle, equipped with a state-of-the-art scope and noise suppressor cradled in his arms, Tony waited patiently for the mark to return home from his usual Thursday night rendezvous with his side bitch. Having done his customary homework on the mark, an investment banker, for several weeks as he always did on all of his intended targets, according to his patterns, this banker always came home late after work on Thursday nights, no later than ten after meeting with his side broad at the Edison hotel on 47th Street in Manhattan. The mark did this every Thursday night like clockwork and would return home afterwards to play the good, faithful husband role with his pregnant wife. In Tony's profession, he understood that every mark has a pattern, and every great hitter has to learn that pattern by doing his homework on that mark. By all standards, Tony was considered a seasoned vet and straight "A" student of the game the consummate professional who knew his craft to an exact science.

Still sitting there patiently and passing the time away waiting for the mark to show up to his date with death, Tony looked at his watch and noticed the time was 9:55 p.m. and thought to himself, *I wonder what kind of lies this investment banker cracker gives his wife every Thursday after creeping with his side pussy. He probably fed her some lame ass shit like,* "honey, I have some extra work to do at the office tonight, so don't wait up. I'll be home late." Or some other lame as shit line like, "honey, don't wait up for me because I'm hanging out at the bar with the fellas tonight." Whatever the lie may have been, the lie, along with that side pussy, was going to be his last.

Looking down at his watch again, it was exactly ten o'clock, so he moved into position. After a couple of minutes had passed, and no signs of the mark, not even so much as a pair of headlights coming up the street, Tony calmly said under his breath, "Where are you, Mr. Investment Banker? You're always on point. You must be putting a little overtime in on the ass or something. Well, I sure hope you enjoy it," he said lowering his rifle. After a few more minutes had passed, he again looked down at his watch. The time was 10:15, and still, no mark.

Growing somewhat impatient, which was uncharacteristic for him, he blurted out, "If I have to stay up here on this roof all muthafuckin' night, I'm finishing this shit!"

Then suddenly, almost as soon as he said that, there were headlights approaching. Assuming it was the mark, Tony quickly moved back into position. As the high beams of the headlights got closer, "*Bingo!*" Tony said out loud, after realizing he was on point.

Just as he guessed, it was the mark, slowly approaching his crib after finally returning home from creeping with his mistress. As the mark pulled into his driveway in his Benz, Tony calmly raised his Rem 700 in the direction of his front door and peered through the high powered night vision scope, in anticipation for the mark moving into the kill zone. Before exiting his ride, the mark turned on the interior light to do some last minute examinations to himself, making sure there was no evidence of his evening rendezvous. After a few more seconds of concealing or destroying any incriminating evidence, the mark stepped out of the car straightening up his suit with one hand and clutching his briefcase with the other hand as he quickly made his way to the front door.

Meanwhile, Tony locked in on him with his trigger finger softly pressing up against the trigger. Standing at the front door, the mark fumbled around with his keys when the door suddenly flung open just as Tony simultaneously squeezed off a shot hitting him in the back underneath his shoulder blade, blowing his heart out of his chest. His lifeless body collapsed forward like a California redwood. His pregnant wife, who had opened the door, fell face first on top of him. Tony suddenly jerked the rifle back from his face in horror and total disbelief. Clutching the rifle, he closed his eyes tightly, hoping that what he just saw wasn't real.

"Fuck! Don't let this shit be happening!" he said out loud. After a brief hesitation, he reluctantly peered back into the scope and his worst fears were realized. He had just violated a major self-imposed rule of his trade. He had accidentally killed an innocent civilian, a pregnant woman lying there face down on top of her husband in a pool of blood. The 7.62mm bullet had travelled straight through the mark and into her.

Suddenly, Tony sprung straight up in the bathtub, sloshing water all over the bathroom floor, awakening from a very surreal nightmare. His heart was racing faster than the bullet that travelled through the mark's body in his dream. Still startled by this nightmare, he sat there for a few minutes trying to regain his composure. Once his rapid heart rate finally returned to normal, it was at this point that Tony finally concluded that what he'd just experienced was more than a recurring nightmare. It was a vision. A prophetic vision. Something that represented more than just a mere dream. The reason being, Tony lived by a strict code which was no hits on women, children, elderly people or other innocent civilians.

However, in this recurring dream, he had accidentally wasted a woman with child, and this would be a cardinal sin in any event, regardless of whether or not it was accidental. In previous dreams he had accidentally shot an old man. In others, he killed the wrong mark and even a child on a merry go round. So after realizing the dreams for what they were, and taking heed to their prophetic overtones, he thus made his mind up right then and there

15

he had to close the chapter on his current profession. To him, now all the idle talk of making a career change was over. It was time for action. So after climbing out of the bathtub and drying off, Tony placed a call to a friend and past business acquaintance, a Colombian cat by the name of Armando Chavez.

Chapter 3

Heeding the Dream

"Hola," a female voice answered in a soft accent.

"Armando por favor," Tony said.

"Si Si, Senor." Seconds later a deep voice answered, "This is Armando speaking."

"Mando! Queue Paso? Tony here."

"Hey Tony, my friend! How are you?"

"Oh, I can't complain, Mando."

"Good! Good, my friend! So what brings this call to Armando? Is everything alright?"

"Yeah everything is good, Mando. I've just decided to take you up on that business proposition you offered me a little while back." Armando laughed.

"So I take it in other words you are ready to become wealthy now?" Tony laughed.

"Yeah, something like that."

"Bueno! Well, my friend, are you ready to take a little vacation anytime soon?"

Tony laughed and asked jokingly, "A vacation? What's that?" Armando let out a hearty laugh into the phone.

"Something that a man who works as hard as you should take every now and then."

"I hear you. Well, Mando, how does this weekend sound?"

"This weekend sounds very good to me, my friend. In fact, Armando will have a limo waiting for you the minute you arrive at the airport."

"Alright, Mando. That's what's up."

"Okay, my friend, Armando will see you soon enough."

Tony slowly placed the phone down on the hook thinking to himself. The prophetic ramifications of his recurring nightmare forced him to be resolute in his departure from a line of work in which he was the consummate professional. But he knew all too well, no matter how good he was at what he did, the real possibility of transgressing his code of no hits on civilians, accidental or otherwise, existed as long as he continued to hunt down marks. The phone call to Armando Chavez marked the beginning of the end of an era and perhaps the beginning of a new profession that was as foreign to him as the country's soil he would soon step foot on for the sole purpose of closing out the era of old. The business proposition that Armando once gave him was one that he could no longer refuse. As those thoughts began to be consumed by the physical and mental strain of the events of the last few hours, the real and the surreal, Tony collapsed on to his satin-sheeted bed, slid his two .45s under his pillow, and copped some much needed rest after a long night at the office.

Chapter 4

Straight Outta Yonkers

Gus' Barber Shop in Crown Heights smelled of old men, ass, Barbasol, and cigar smoke. The shop's old jukebox speakers blared *My Man Don't Love Me* by Billie Holiday, while the old timers engaged in spirited topics that ranged from Lady Day herself to the 1919 World Series and who fixed it, to the Kennedy and MLK assassinations, even though this was the year 2015. They were even in a heated discussion with some young cat about how Sugar Ray Robinson would whip the shit out Floyd *Money* Mayweather. It was as if this barber shop was stuck in a time warp. But just like any black-owned barber shop, it was common knowledge throughout America that it is a place of controversy, man gossip, half-truths, no truths, outright lies, embellished stories, and spirited debates that normally involved the typical negroisms. One would also find in any black barbershop in America, the typical neighborhood brats left by their mothers, looking to catch a break, wreaking havoc, while the older folks levied empty threats against them. This day at the barbershop was no different. As the loud chatter among the shop's patrons, barbers and some of the youngsters went on, Tony sat there with an amused look on his face while peering down at an old, outdated 1973 issue of Jet magazine with the lovely Jane Kennedy gracing its front cover. Yes, 1973. For the younger cats who didn't know Jane Kennedy and would question why her issue would still be floating around the shop decades later, the old folks would use it as a little history lesson. By the time they left, the young men would know that she was the first black female sportscaster and also one of the first celebrities, black or white, to make a very infamous sex tape with her actor husband, Isaac Kennedy of the old school penitentiary movies.

When the only young teenage jit in the shop walked to the jukebox and didn't see any up to date music, he began to protest.

"Maaaaaaaan, why y'all ain't got no up to date artists in here?" he asked with contempt. "Y'all need to get some Yung Thug, Jeezy or Plies up in this bitch. Y'all can at least have some Tupac."

"You watch your mouth up in here, youngster," one of the barbers admonished him.

"We don't have that bullshit in here for a reason, son," another barber said. The youngster rolled his eyes and sucked his teeth as he continued to stand there at the jukebox looking for an artist of his era. "That gangsta rap shit is partly what's wrong with you young niggas' generation. If y'all listened to artists like the Temptations, the Delfonics and Marvin Gaye that sing about love and social consciousness, maybe y'all wouldn't be 'round here killing each other and calling your women bitches and hoes."

The other old timers sounded off in agreement like they were in church. But everything they were saying fell on deaf ears. The youngster just continued to stand there at the jukebox with the typical defiant young person look on his face. To him, these old timers were speaking Mandarin Chinese or speaking in tongues. He didn't understand *none* of that shit and he wasn't trying to hear *none* of that shit. After hearing enough of the lecturing and preaching that he got more than enough of at the crib from his ma dukes, the youngster headed for the door.

As he was leaving, one of the barbers yelled to him, "*And pull up yo goddamn pants! Don't nobody wanna see your ass crack and streak marks.*" With one final act of defiance, the youngster threw up the middle finger as he exited the shop.

By the time Tony sat down in the barber's chair, two men wearing bomber jackets and Timberland boots walked in and sat down. One appeared to have already had a fresh cut and the other

20

who wore his hair in dreads, looked like his had been freshly done also. Their faces were stone cold. A third man who had walked up with them, but suddenly peeled off from them once they reached the barbershop, stood outside with his hands in his pocket chain smoking and nervously scanning the streets back and forth as if his head was one of those oscillating fans. Strange enough, it was at least 20 degrees and dropping outside which was the reason the few people who braved the weather, were scurrying to get where they were going with no delay. The other people who stood around in that hawk, were the typical junkies, of course, but even they had enough sense to stand huddled up around the barrel fires to keep themselves warm. But this dude who smoked more than a busted chimney, just stood there with his hands in his pockets.

"What will it be this time, Stall, the usual?" the barber asked Tony.

"Yep. The usual, Gus. Just give me a ball fade, and knock down the loose ends on the top and keep this beard sharp as a knife."

"Ok. The usual, coming up," Gus said as he tied the barber tape around Tony's neck.

As Gus put his guards on his clippers, the little brats' mother, a tall, brown-skinned, beautiful sister who had the look of a stripper slash ho, walked in and paid the barber for their haircuts before exiting with all five in line behind her like Mother Goose.

"Gaaawwd damn! I'm glad those lil' bastards are gone!" one of the old timer barbers said. "Muthafuckas don't have no kinda home training. Hell, I bet all of 'em got different pappies, too," he added, shaking his head as he swept the floor furiously.

"You bet not let their mother hear you say that shit about her kids, Joe. You know she's a known cutter. She'll cut your old ass too short to shit. You know the whore is crazy. She once sliced up her pimp she was working for."

"Yeah, I know that bitch crazy because her crumb snatchers are retarded. I bet all of 'em catch the lil' short yellow bus to school. Anybody that goddamn bad gotta be in special ed."

The barbershop broke out in laughter, all except for the two men who had just walked in. They didn't crack a smile or break their gaze. They just continued to sit there stone-faced and looking out of place. The third guy who chose to stand outside and brave the cold, for some unknown reason, moved across the street to the fire barrel to partake in some warmth next to the junkies.

"Yeah, I heard every one of those lil' bastards are trick babies," Joe continued on. "You see the two high yellow ones with the freckles and the blue eyes? I know goddamn well they some honky's babies. Probably the milk man's babies."

The barbershop once again erupted into laughter, with the exception of the two stone-faced men. They either didn't seem to have a sense of humor or they had something far more pressing and serious on their minds that was of no laughing matter.

"Come to think of it, those two lil' half breeds look like that cracker Stanley Cranston, the insurance man who be making rounds in this area."

"Awwww, Joe, cut that shit out," Gus said. "Those kids' aren't Stanley's kids. Their father is that assistant district attorney Franks."

"You shitting me!" Joe said looking over his spectacles in surprise.

"Yeah, Joe, that's old news, just like your old ass." This caused more laughter to break out.

"You must be getting old and senile 'cause everybody knew their mother was tricking with Franks. In fact, Honey, is a top dollar whore."

"Oh ok. No damn wonder she wouldn't let me buy no pussy off her," Joe said with contempt. "I tried to give the hooker *fifty whole dollars* and she laughed at me."

"Of course she laughed at your little fifty dollars when she be getting four and five hundred dollars a trick. You couldn't even get a hand job from her for fifty dollars, Joe. Did you see what she drove up in?"

"Naw. I thought the bitch rode up here on a bicycle." This caused another round of laughter from the patrons, even Tony snickered at that one. The two cats who had just walked in however, they didn't crack a smile. Their lack of a sense of humor, no one picked up on, because it wasn't uncommon for Brooklyn. Therefore, no one in the barbershop seemed to pay them any attention....except for Tony.

"Nah, try again," Gus said.

"A go cart?" Joe quipped, causing more laughter.

"*No man!* She drove up here in something that's worth more than your old broke down ass, a brand new Benz, and she also drives an imported Porsche."

"Yeah, and with all them damn chullins she need to trade both of them in for a school bus. No damn wonder she didn't want my fifty dollars then. I guess I will just stick to the ten dollar pussy. Hell, if I pay a bitch five hundred dollars, she gone have to give me pussy for a whole year, cook me three meals a day and wipe my ass when I shit."

Once again, the barbershop broke out into laughter, including Tony who let out a couple of chuckles at this old timer who was just as cantankerous as Fred Sanford, and just as funny. However, no matter how funny the old man was, the two cats never broke a smile, a laugh, not even a grin. They remained stone-faced throughout. One of the barbers finally took noticed of them when it appeared that neither one of the guys needed a haircut.

"Hey, any one of you gentlemen next?" one of the barbers who had just finished a cut, asked them. Before answering they hesitated as if the question caught them off guard.

"Uh, no sir. We waiting on him," one of them said pointing at Gus.

"Oh, ok. So y'all waiting on Gus," the barber said. Joe then peered at them over his glasses and said, "Son, you look like you just had a fresh cut. Where y'all from? I've never seen y'all around here before." Both looked at him as if he said something about their mothers.

"We're from Harlem," one of them quickly answered.

"They don't have barbershops in Harlem?" Joe asked.

"Y'all came all the way over to Crown Heights just to get a cut?" Gus intervened.

"Joe, why are you being so damn nosey? It ain't none of your damn business why these gentlemen decided to get a cut here. I done told your old ass to stop sticking your nose in other folks business. Somebody gonna shoot it off one of these days."

"Well, I'm just asking a question, Gus. *Damn!* I just it find it rather odd they came all the way over here to get a cut, especially when they look like they just had one today."

"Ok, but that's their own business if they want it cut again. Leave folks alone, man."

"Alright, Gus. Shit! Don't make me go in my back pocket 'cause if I do yo ass won't leave up outta here without a cut on it." The barbershop broke out again into laughter.

"Yeah, ok. I wish you would pull that old rusty ass knife out on me. I'll make you cut your *god damn* self with it." Everyone, including Tony, started laughing again. One of the two cats did manage to crack a slight grin this time. Perhaps he was trying to allay anymore suspicion.

"Well, I guess I'll take off to the house now before I have to hurt somebody up in here," Joe said, shutting down his station.

"Yeah, take your old ass on home," one of the other barbers said.

"That's just what I'm about to do, but not because your *old* ass telling me too. I have a date tonight with a young gal."

"Oh, yeah?" Gus asked.

"Yes sir. I have a date with a fine ass young tender thang."

"Alright now. You just make sure you take your nitroglycerin so you don't have no heart attack fucking with that young gal," Gus said.

"Hell, he gotta get it up first before he can have a heart attack," the other barber said. This caused another round of laughter.

"Awww fuck you!" Joe responded. "Everything on me still work good, muthafucka. Ask your momma. She'll tell you how good everything still work." Everyone burst out laughing again. Mumbling to himself just like Fred Sanford, Joe grabbed his coat, hat and cane and walked out of the shop. He even walked like Fred Sanford.

"Hey, Graham. You shouldn't have said that," Gus said laughing. "You know Joe gotta take Viagra and use a penis pump to get it up."

"Really? Gus, you lying?" Graham said as he paused on cutting his customer's head.

"Yeah, really," Gus said laughing.

"Well, damn! I was just fucking with him. How did I know he gotta pump his dick up?" he said as more laughter erupted all except from the two Harlem niggas. They remained there in the same spot, in the same posture, and with the same units on their faces.

After the last customer sat down in the barber's chair two chairs over from Gus, one of the two cats strolled to the bathroom while the other remained seated. Tony not once looking up, kept his eyes fixed on that same Jet magazine he had been sifting through from the moment he sat down in barber's chair which was going on an hour now. Gus, who was considered by many to

be the best barber in Brooklyn, was also renowned for being no-
toriously slow. However, those like Tony who had an appreciation for a good quality hair cut, didn't view Gus as being slow,
but rather the meticulousness of an artist or an architect paying
close attention to detail in his craft. Those were the type of traits
that a cat like Tony could respect, since he too possessed those
same traits, but in a different game.

A couple of minutes later, the tall lanky cat with braids
emerged from the restroom and sat back down in his seat as his
partner immediately got right up and went to the restroom. Seemingly oblivious to the two men's furtive movements, Tony continued on looking at the magazine. A couple minutes later the
Harlem cat emerged from the restroom and sat back down in front
of Tony who still did not break his gaze from the magazine.

When the last customer climbed from the barber's chair,
and the last remaining barber brushed the loose excess hairs from
his head and clothes, the silver haired gentleman paid him,
grabbed his old man derby and coat then exited the shop to brave
the cold outside. At this point, Gus was putting the finishing
touches on Tony's razor sharp sideburns. It was also at this point
that one of the Harlem cats popped up from his chair and locked
the shop's door. The third cat who had been outside in the hawk,
trotted across the street with his hands in his pockets and posted
back up in front of the shop.

"Hey, son. Who told you to lock that door? We're not closed
yet." Gus asked, looking over his glasses.

"Yeah well, you closed now, old man," he said.

"What is that supposed to mean? I know damn well you two
young niggas ain't planning on sticking this place up. We don't
carry a lot of cash here."

"Pops, chill the fuck out and rest your nerves before you have
a stroke. We didn't come all the way from Yonkers to lay your
old ass down, because we ain't on some petty ass shit like that.

26

We came here for more important reasons," he said, smiling as he and his partner reached into their bomber jackets and pulled strap.

"Well, if you didn't come here to lay us down, what are you here for, son? And why the guns?"

"I think Mr. Stallworth know what we're here for, don't you O.G.?" he said, smiling.

"No jit," Tony responded. "I don't have the slightest idea why you are here, but I'm sure you will soon fill me in on it." Laughing, the young gangsta walked in front of Tony shaking his head with the Glock 40 in his hand.

"Now, Mr. Stallworth, I'm a little disappointed in you. You must be getting old, because you slipping. Two suspect niggas walk in here with a third standing outside in that cold ass weather and you wonder why we here? *Really?* Again, I'm disappointed in you, O.G., after hearing so much gangsta shit about you," he said as he motioned to his partner to close the blinds.

"Well, I'm flattered that you've heard so much about me and I'm dismayed that I disappointed you, but that still doesn't answer my question. Why have you and your partner come all the way from Harlem to pay me a visit?"

"Yonkers. We came from Yonkers," he responded.

"Okay. Why did you come all the way from Yonkers to see me?"

"Well, let's just say we got business with you. Compliments of a friend of a rich friend," he said, grinning wickedly from ear to ear. He then raised his tool and asked, "Okay. Now to this business. Where you want it? The chest or the head?"

"Wow! Since you are kind enough to give me a choice in the matter, I guess in the chest so my folks can have an open casket at my home going service."

The two killers from Yonkers broke out in laughter. "I almost hate to kill this nigga," he turned and said to his partner.

27

"Okay, old man," he said, motioning his gun at Gus. "I think you better step to the side."

"Wait a minute, son. Look!" Gus said with his hands in front of him shielding Tony. "You don't have to do this! Aren't there enough of you young brothers already dying in this city?"

"Listen, pops! This nigga here in your chair has done his own share of killing in this city and elsewhere. Did you know that? A few months ago in Manhattan, he murked the brother of the man who sent me here." Gus looked at Tony in surprise. "Yeah that's right. Mr. Stallworth here is a killer for scriller. He be putting in that work. A cold blooded killer at that. One of the best. In fact, before I had this business on him, he was my hero. Now pops, like I said, if you don't wanna get shot, I suggest you move over a couple feet next to the other barber. I only got business with Mr. Stallworth, but a bullet doesn't have just his name written on it."

Not wanting to get shot, Gus reluctantly complied and meandered over to the other side of the barbershop out of the line of fire as he looked back at Tony, a man he's known since his uncle used to bring him in as a youngster to get his haircut.

"Okay now, Mr. Stallworth, I'm gonna need you to stand up. I have a real problem with shooting a nigga while he's sitting down."

"A killer with rules. I can respect that," Tony said smiling.

"Yeah, Mr. Stallworth, I guess you can say I'm extending you a little professional courtesy. One killer for scriller to another. Now stand up. But do it *slowly*." As Tony began to stand up, the two killers bodies seem to tense up with nervousness or perhaps with excitement of the prospect of a kill. As soon as Tony stood fully erect, and before his would be killer could take aim, an explosion ripped clean through Tony's barber's gown and the Jet magazine he was still holding. The bullet traveled through Jane's naval and struck the young hitter sending him sliding under the rows of chairs. Another quick explosion immediately followed from the pistol in Tony's left hand, then another from the pistol in the right hand that hit the second cat, knocking him into the wall, causing him to fire off his Glock wildly into the ceiling as Gus and the other barber hit the floor and began frantically scrambling and crawling out of the line of fire. Casually walking forward a couple of steps with both gold plated .45s steadily trained directly on the wounded gunman, Tony let off two more shots into him that lifted his body off the floor with each shot that ceased all movement. After making sure he was dead, and kicking his gun clean to the other side of the room, Tony turned his attention to the third lookout outside. When he peeped out of the shop's blinds, all he saw was the lookout making a mad dash down the sidewalk bumping and nudging the people he passed. Dude was running so fast he had to hold down his ball cap on his head to keep from losing it.

"Y'all alright, Gus?" Tony asked.

"Yeah, Stall. Other than a little shit in our pants, we're okay," he said. The other barber who couldn't speak, perhaps from shock, was still on the floor trembling like he had Parkinson's disease. Over in the corner, the remaining killer began to moan and writhe in pain. He attempted to move his legs, but they refused to cooperate with him. One of the shots that hit him, traveled straight through the middle of his chest, severing his spinal cord, and exited his back into the wall. There were blood splatters, blood smears, spinal fluid, and bone fragments covering parts of the wall and on the floor where he had slid under the chairs leaving a greasy streak. Not taking any chances, Tony cautiously walked over and kicked his gun away. Kneeling over the Y.G. who couldn't have been any more than 20, Tony asked, "Now will you finally tell me exactly why you paid me this visit?" Steady coughing up blood, he mustered up enough strength to respond.

"It don't even matter now, do it?" he said. Tony shook his head.

"Nah. I guess not, jit," he said softly.

"You're a baaaaaaaaaaaaad man," the youngster said smiling as he began to cough up more blood. A few seconds later, this young aspiring killer from Yonkers took his last breath as Tony knelt over him, frozen in place. He was obviously shook up over having to kill this young jit, although he was there to do the same to him. As the sirens approached, which was Tony's cue to tear out from the scene, he turned and profusely apologized to Gus and the other barber before slipping out the back exit. This regrettable incident struck an emotional chord with Tony like no other. Not because he was forced to take a life to defend his own which he had done dozens of times over the course of his life, but because of the age of the young man. A promising young man who, other than the amateurish moves of putting in work in front of witnesses and worst yet, announcing himself and broadcasting his intentions, Tony couldn't help but to see himself in this jit. In fact, 15 years earlier, Tony *was* this jit. However, there is an immutable law in the universe that governs the instincts of animals and humans alike, you either kill or be killed. Today, Tony was forced to adhere to and obey that law.

Chapter 5

The Stranger From Up the Block

Casually walking his white Tibetan Mastiff, a slim, blinged out, old man dressed in a burgundy and black smoking jacket, and who had the look of wealth and sophistication, took short puffs from his cigar in the park. The Mastiff, a hulking figure of a dog that easily outweighed his master, patiently walked beside him, although he could have very easily drug him all over the park if he'd chosen to. This dog was obviously trained to be obedient to his master's commands. When his master walked, he too walked. When his master stopped to puff on that Cuban cigar in the corner of his mouth, the huge animal stopped dead in his tracks to await the next move.

About 100 feet away, was a white man wearing shades and standing next to a bench with his right foot propped up on it as he peered around the park while talking on his cell phone. He looked like a cop who was trying to be inconspicuous, but was doing a poor job of it. Another gentleman, also wearing shades, stood leaning up against a pearl black Rolls Royce limo. He too had the look of a cop, but one who had been in one too many bar fights. Just like the other gentleman, he also stood there as if he was just passing the time away. After finishing the last of his cigar, and discarding it in the sandbox where the dogs take their shit, the man headed towards the black limo with his beast walking alongside of him, seemingly in lock step. The other man who was posted up near the bench began trailing him and making his way to the limo as he scanned the area cautiously from east to west. It was obvious this slender elderly gentleman with the high priced show dog was an important man. Why else would he have a couple of trained overseers flanking him?

After climbing into the back seat of the limo with his dog, the old man said to the driver, "Hey Charlie, I need you to pull into Katz Delicatessen on the way back. I have a taste for one of those Reuben sandwiches."

"Okay boss," the hulking driver said in a deep voice. Katz Delicatessen, a Jewish spot, was one of the oldest in New York. In fact, the famous scene from the movie *When Harry Met Sally* where Meg Ryan's character faked an orgasm, was filmed inside Katz's. Many a big shot gangster, politician, musician, celebrity and square alike frequented Katz.

When the limo pulled up to the curve, the old man gave the driver a $20. "Grab me one of those Reubens, and tell them to put extra Thousand Island dressing on it this time. Get you and Mo something, too, if you like, Charlie."

While the driver went inside to retrieve the food, the bodyguard, Mo, stepped out of the limo for a quick smoke. Across the street, about a block away, a tall slender black man wearing shades and a New York Yankees ball cap pulled down over his head waited for the pedestrian sign to change so he could cross the street.

While he waited on his bodyguard to return with his food, the old man sat in the back of the limo rubbing his dog's head.

"We'll be going home in a minute, boy," he said. "Pappa gotta get something to eat. Are you getting hungry too?" he asked the dog who looked as though he understood every word his master was saying to him. The dog let out a bark. "Yes, I know, boy. Pappa knows you're hungry. We will be home in a minute, where I have a big juicy Porterhouse Steak waiting on you," the old man said, looking the dog in his eyes and rubbing his head.

"Woof! Woof! Woof!" the huge Mastiff responded back, causing the limo to shake with each thunderous bark. Meanwhile, Mo continued to walk aimlessly alongside the limo still puffing on the cigarette.

"Hey, Mo."

"Yes sir," Mo said, peeping his head inside the limo's front driver side window.

"I almost forgot. Can you run in there and order an extra Reuben? My Mattie would kill me if I brought back something from her favorite deli and didn't bring her anything. Here you go. An extra ten spot should cover it."

"Okay sir. Sure thing." Mo responded before heading towards the deli.

"Mo, make sure you grab you something too, if you're hungry," the old man yelled.

"Will do, sir. Thank you," he said before walking inside Katz. By the time Mo was going in, Charlie, the driver, was coming out which at the time the black man with dreads, wearing a Bob Marley shirt and Yankee ball cap had made his way down the sidewalk connected to the curve the limo sat parked on.

"Alright, Charlie, did they make sure they added the extra dressing this time?"

"Yes sir. In fact, they put extra on the sandwich and extra on the side. I told the owner whom the order was for and he gave it to you on the house. He said it was his compliments since the last sandwich didn't have extra dressing."

"Oh did he?" the old man said. "He didn't have to do that. Did you tip him?"

"Yes sir. I tipped him out of my own money." Charlie said as handed his boss back his $20 bill.

"Wow! That Jacob is a real class act. He's a Jew, but nonetheless as good as they come. Hey Charlie, run back inside and tell him to peep his head out, so I can say hello."

"Sure thing, sir." Charlie climbed out of the limo.

When Charlie walked inside, the tall black man wearing the Yankee ball cap tapped on the window and said to the old man,

"Nice dog you have there." Not making out what he said, the old man cracked his window.

"What was that, fella?" he asked as the thunderous barks of the dog began shaking the limo.

"I said, nice dog. I had a red one just like it." The old man chuckled as he tried to contain the beast. "You had a dog like this one, you say?"

"Yes sir."

"Okay fella. If you say so. This dog cost me fifty grand, and that was a discount because I'm friends with the breeder."

"I'm familiar with the breed, sir," the stranger said smiling. He recognized the white man's attitude that suggested a black man isn't supposed to have knowledge of a dog of that breed, let alone afford to own one. "This particular breed doesn't shed. They are strong-willed, loyal, tenacious, and the bloodline that you have came from Tibet. His grandfather's name was Zhang Gengyun who derived from the same line as the pair owned by King George IV of England."

"Wow. I'm impressed. You do seem to know your dog breeds."

"Oh yeah. I do know my dog breeds." the man said, laughing. "You know what else I know?"

"What's that, fella?" the old man asked with a bewildered look.

"I'm also familiar with the man who sold this beautiful beast to you." The old man frowned.

"Who the hell are you?" he asked in a panicked voice.

"Who am I? I'm the man you sent that youngster to pay me a visit who hadn't begun to live his life yet," the stranger said harshly. The old man frantically rolled up the window as the dog barked wildly. The stranger just stood there smiling, and shaking his head in total disgust as he watched the old man struggle to stretch his body out to reach for the horn to alert his men at which time the stranger disappeared. In an attempt to locate him, the old man looked around on each side of the vehicle, with wide stretched eyes, but could not see him. Turning his body completely around in the seat to see if he could locate him, the old man spotted him behind the car a short distance away, smiling and waving at him with something in his right hand that he couldn't make out due to his poor vision.

Once the stranger pulled a pin from the object he held in his hand and rolled it under the limo as if he was bowling, the old man, a Korean War combat vet, knew exactly what it was.

"Grenade!" he screamed, seeming to have a flashback from the war as he scrambled in vain to get out of the limo, while the Mastiff barked incessantly. Standing inside the deli, Mo saw his boss' ordeal, but before he could rush to his rescue, the limo exploded into a huge fireball, lifting it up off the pavement and shattered Katz's windows, sending the employees and handful of customers scuffling to the floor. One of the limo's hubcaps was lodged deep into the front wall of the restaurant, and what was left of the old man was protruding halfway through the front of the blown out windshield. Not surprisingly, his fifty thousand dollar beast was still alive, but barely. Part of the steering wheel was impaled through his massive torso as his lifeblood steadily drained out through the gaping hole in the floorboard and out onto the street.

The terrified bystanders scrambled away from the limo for dear life, perhaps fearing a secondary explosion. A shocked Mo and Charlie walked outside in total disbelief at what they saw. Perhaps a part of them were relieved that they didn't go with their boss. Just a few more seconds and they would have been inside the car with him, splattered all over the streets.

The stranger casually flagged down the cab parked on the corner of the block, and hopped in.

"I'm going to Park Slope," he said to the cab driver. As the cab sped away, Tony looked straight ahead as if nothing happened as the radio played *Da Last Real Nigga Left* by Plies.

Chapter 6

Angela Washington

At 6 a.m. sharp, Tony began his daily morning workout which consisted of a five mile jog, a rigorous weight lifting session, a few rounds on the heavy bag, and target practice in his sound proof room behind his crib. Staying in supreme physical condition and maintaining the lethal skills of his soon-to-be former trade had become ritualistic for Tony over the years. Soon after finishing up his workout, Tony listened to his new state of the art answering machine while he prepared a nutritional cocktail to put the electrolytes and nutrients back into his body.

"Hey Tony. This is Angela. I see you're still missing in action, *once again.* I've called you several times already, but you haven't returned any of my calls. Sooooo, anyway, whenever you decide to return my calls, I'll be here like always. Take care, Tony." Recognizing the frustration and disappointment in her voice, Tony quickly downed his cocktail and returned her call. Angela was a woman Tony cared a great deal for and would perhaps take for his wife and have a family with, if it were not for his profession. Tony was well aware of the fact Angela was madly in love with him, and would perhaps accept what he did for a living and be with him no matter what. However, he could not bring himself to take on a liability in his risky and dangerous profession and therefore did not allow their relationship to extend beyond the dating level, which had been on and off for the past five to six years.

"Hello! This is Angela speaking."

"Hey, Angela. This is Tony. How are you, baby?"

"Tony? Tony who? Do I know you or something, sir?" Tony laughed out loud.

"Okay. Okay. I'm sorry, baby."

"Sorry? What are you sorry for, sir?"

Still laughing profusely he said, "Sorry for not promptly returning your calls, Miss Washington. So would you pleeeze accept my deepest apologies, ma'am?"

"Well...Well...I guess I can."

"What do you mean you guess you can?" Tony said, laughing even harder. "You know it's in your nature. In fact, you are the sweetest woman I know." Though he would never admit to it, he at times took Angela for granted. Like most cats who felt they had enough swag to get any broad they wanted, he was under the belief that Angela would always be there.

"Yeah, yeah, ummm hmmm. I know. And that's what you count on too when you know you've done wrong. I tell you, Mr. Stallworth, you're gonna mess right around one of these days and turn me into scorned woman."

"Oh no!" he said, laughing. "Not the scorned, angry black woman? Well, we certainly can't have that, now can we? So can I please make it up to you by taking you out to dinner tonight at a nice authentic Italian restaurant?"

"Well, I don't know...let me check my schedule. I may just already have a date lined up."

"Woman, would you just please let me kiss your perfectly round bottom tonight, alright?"

Finally relenting, she laughed and said, "Okay, Mr. Stallworth. But you had better do a damn good job of kissing this ass tonight!"

Tony nearly dropped the phone he laughed so hard. After composing himself he said, "Alright, Miss Washington. Alright. See you at six sharp, baby."

"No! See you at 5:59, Mr. Stallworth."

"Okay, baby, 5:59 it is." After hanging up, Tony stood there at the bar for a moment shaking his head smiling before turning on the eight track and heading to the shower. The song *La La Means I Love You* by the Delfonics blared from the speakers.

Later that evening at exactly 5:58, Tony pulled up in Angela's driveway and lightly honked the horn. A beautiful face peeped out of the curtains and motioned to him to give her a second. Minutes later she appeared wearing a blood red dress that conservatively revealed her petite, well-constructed frame. Tony immediately jumped from his ride and tilted his dark blue gangster hat to her before he opened the passenger door all gentlemanly for her to get in. She chuckled like a teenage girl.

"Why thank you, sir, that's very gentlemanly of you." Tony laughed and closed her door. After climbing into the driver's seat, he leaned over and placed a soft kiss on her cheek.

"Baby, you look absolutely gorgeous tonight," he said. She gave him a wide toothy smile followed by an incredulous look as if to say, *nigga, please. You're gonna have to do more than flatter me tonight with compliments I've heard before a thousand times.*

"Why thank you, Mr. Stallworth," she said facetiously. "And I see you're off to a good start tonight on your ass kissing mission. Smart man." They both laughed out loud as they headed off on their dinner date.

Twenty minutes later they arrived at Michael's over in Marine Park in Brooklyn. This spot was one of the most popular Italian restaurants in the city, and Angela's favorite. This spot had the look and feel of an Italian village. The exterior was built with rusticated stone, which made it look like one of those hilltop fortresses in old Italy. The interior was bedecked in chandeliers and paneled in warm wood and waiters wearing tuxedos. The music coming from the large banquet room was *I Got You Under My Skin* by old Blue Eyes himself, Frank Sinatra, who was said to frequent this spot, which had the look of one of those old gangster movies.

"Hello, Ms. Washington. How are you this evening?"

"I'm fine, Sergio. And yourself?"

"Been a little hectic in here tonight. Other than that, all is well."

"Okay. Great. This is my boyfriend, Tony."

"Boyfriend? Wow! I didn't know you were taken since you are always in here alone. Hello, Tony, how are you?" he said, before shaking Tony's hand.

"I'm good. Nice to meet you too, player." Tony smiled.

"Yes. I have had a man all this time." Angela said, smiling. "And I thought I told you that?"

"Yes. I do recall you telling me that once. But I've never seen anyone with you other than those old men from your job. Well, anyway, again Tony, nice to meet you."

"Likewise," Tony said, smiling and cutting his eyes over at Angela.

"So, what are you two having to drink tonight? This is our wine list here," he said, placing the list down on the table. "As you already know, Angela, all our wines are made in Italy and imported here specifically for this restaurant."

"Yes, I know. But you already know I want the usual."

"Okay. Sangria it is. And you, Tony? What will you have?"

"I will just take a hot tea with a lemon wedge."

"Okay. One hot tea for the boyfriend, and one Sangria for the lady coming right up. Be right back with your beverages."

"So you are a regular here, I take it." Tony said, smiling.

"Something like that. I've been coming here since it opened. The owners are from the same town, Palermo, where my mother is from."

"Oh yeah?" Tony said. "Small world. What about dude?"

"What about him?" she asked.

"He seemed a little caught off guard when you introduced me as your man."

"Oh," she said, smiling. "Yeah that would catch him off guard."

"And why is that?" he asked, monitoring her eyes.

"Well, because he and I dated briefly before I broke it off with him. Since then he's been trying to get back in."

"Ohhhhh ok. That explains it."

"That explains what?"

"That explains the look in his eyes when you broke it to him that I'm that dude." Tony smirked.

"Oh wait a minute, Mr. Stallworth. It wasn't like that. We dated for one month which means *nothing* happened."

"Hold on. I wasn't implying that," he said smiling.

"Oh cut it out. I know where you were going with that." Tony laughed.

"No. No. No. I swear I wasn't going there. I know what kind of woman you are."

"Ummm hmm," she said, smiling. Part of her kind of enjoyed the prospect of Tony being jealous of Sergio. Although he'd never really shown jealousy in the past, she believed on occasions that he was.

"Okay. One Sangria and one hot tea. Be careful. That tea is piping hot, Mr. Tony. Okay, are we ready to order now? Angela, I think I already know what you want."

"Nah. I'm going to change it up this time," she said.

"Ohhhh. Okay. You're just changing up everything." He gave a phony laugh.

"Yes. Change is good," she fired back. Appearing amused, Tony sipped on his tea. "I'm going to have the Veal Piccata over Angel Hair and Parmigiana Reggiano."

"Okay. Gotcha. And you, Mr. Tony? What are you having tonight?"

"I'm going to have the Linguini with white clam sauce."

"Ohhh. You sound like you're familiar with Italian cuisine. And didn't even have to look at the menu. I'm impressed." Tony smirked.

"Vuoi che ti dia il mio ordine in italiano? Avrò la Linguine con vongole bianco."

"Oh wow! You even speak fluent Italian," he said with a shit eating grin. Angela sat back in her seat sipping on her Sangria. To say she was amused was an understatement. She was being downright entertained like a Queen watching her King handle the jester.

Not trying to stall him out, Tony leaned forward and said, "Oh ho visto? Tu non parli italiano? Opps. I mean, you don't understand Italian? My apologies. But aren't you Italian, Serg?"

"He he he," he laughed sheepishly. "Well, like Angela, my mother is Italian. My father is an American white man from the south who objected to his children learning to speak Italian. Said it was un-American," he said with a disappointed look on his face. "Well, let me go ahead and put in you guys orders. Shouldn't take too long."

After the waiter walked off to the kitchen, Tony sipped on his tea and peered over at Angela. "Poor fellow," he said.

"You can be vicious sometimes. You do know that, don't you?" she said with a chuckle.

"Yes, I've been told that a time or two over the course of my life. But you liked every minute of my viciousness here tonight, didn't you?"

"Yes. I won't lie. Not only did I like it. It turned me on. You were kind of hot speaking Italian like that." Tony laughed and sipped his tea.

"Well, I learned from a good teacher."

"Is that right?" she said.

"That's right. You are the best teacher I ever had."

"Ummmm okay. Well, why have I never received my shiny red apple from you, then?"

"I never took you for the shiny red apple type."

"You already know, red is my favorite color. But you are right. I hate apples. They get stuck in my teeth." They both laughed aloud. A few seconds later, Sergio returned with their food on a huge serving tray.

"Okay here you are, Ms. Washington. Your Veal Picatta over Angela Hair and Parmigiana Reggiano. And Mr. Tony, here's your Linguini with white clam sauce. Looks good! Can I get you guys anything else this evening?"

"No, I'm good," said Angela."

"I'm good, too, Sergio. This is more than enough. Thank you."

"Okay. Well, if you guys need anything else, don't hesitate to ask." Sergio walked off to the next table of customers.

"Wow! I've never seen him this humbled," Angela said smiling.

"Ole Serg is alright. We just had to get a little male understanding." He smiled. "Damn! That really looks good, Angela. I should have ordered that instead."

"Really, Tony? Now you know you don't eat red meat."

"I know. But tonight I would make an exception. That really looks delicious."

"Oh stop it! You haven't eaten land animals in ten years. If you ate one bite of this it would surely make you ill."

"I *know* it would make me ill. But it would be well worth a tore up stomach." They both laughed.

Not long after finishing their dinner, Tony mentioned his plans to make a career change. From the beginning of their relationship, Tony had long ago fed Angela a line of bullshit that he was this big time traveling salesman which was partly true. But of course he didn't dare tell her, or anyone else for that matter, what he truly sold, death.

"Well, what do you plan to do when you get out of the sales business, Tony?" Tony sipped on his hot tea and calmly rolled a smooth lie off his lips without missing a beat.

"Foreign imports." He braced for the next inevitable question.

She took a sip of her Sangria. "Ummm hmmm. What kind of imports, baby?"

Damn! Tony thought to himself. *I figured that would be your very next question.* "Well, I'm not exactly sure as of yet, baby, but I'm currently looking at some very attractive markets. Do you know of any or have some suggestions?" *I sure hope that turned the tables on the third degree,* he thought to himself as he continued sipping on his tea.

"Well sure, Tony. As a matter of fact, the textile market is a very profitable market right now. In fact, countries like China, Pakistan, and Turkey are textile nations that are extremely good nations to import from. The reason being, anywhere the American dollar is dominant over another country's currency, that is the country you want to import from."

"Is that right?" he smiled and thought to himself, *I was actually thinking more of importing from a country like, let's saaaaay, Bogota, Columbia.*

Taking another short sip of her Sangria, she stared at him, as if to monitor him carefully. "Tony, what's on your mind right now?" she asked.

Reaching across the table and gently grabbing her hand, he said in a smooth voice, "I was just sitting here admiring what a beautiful piece of work God put together when he created you."

Blushing, she said, "Flattery will get you everywhere with me tonight, Mr. Stallworth."

Bringing her soft hand up to his lips, Tony kissed it softly, and then ran his tongue between her fingers and on her long red fingernails until she started to moan and close her eyes. Feeling the effects of the Sangria and Tony's tongue, she opened her eyes slowly and said in a low exasperated voice, "It's time for us to go now, Mr. Stallworth." Tony momentarily stared into her eyes. He knew all too well the look that read "Let's go home and fuck until we collapse from exhaustion." For he'd seen that look in her eyes too many times over the years not to recognize it. So after paying Serg, the waiter, Tony took her to her crib.

Before Tony and Angela could get in the house good, they began kissing and undressing each other, all the while, not saying a word. Angela, who wore a conservative veneer in public, was the classic freak bitch in private.

Not missing a beat, Tony pushed the door closed as they continued to kiss passionately. Right there at the door, Angela dropped to her knees and unzipped his pants. Looking up at him with an innocent school girl look, she clutched his dick with her hands, pulled it out, and began sucking it softly. Engulfed in pure pleasure, Tony's eyes rolled back and his knees became weak. After a few moments of Angela's skilled head game, Tony couldn't take it anymore. He scooped her up into his arms and began kissing her wildly as he carried her into her bedroom, where he laid her down gently on the edge of her bed.

Angela turned over onto her stomach with her head facing his crotch, placed her hand gently on his rock hard dick with one hand and, with the other hand, softly cuffed his balls and commenced putting in more work. Super Head had nothing on her. Tony stood there at attention with his head tilted downwards, looking at her voluptuous lips sliding, with ease, up and down on his big shiny dick that was drenched from her saliva. Every couple of seconds, she would slide it inside her jaw and each time she brought it out from the corner of her mouth it would make a popping sound that echoed all over the room. She would then move her moist tongue up and in a circular motion around the head of his dick while her eyes stayed locked on his. When she concluded her masterful head session, Tony, then fell to his knees right there at the edge of the bed with the intentions of returning the favor.

As if she could read his mind, Angela turned over onto her back and slowly opened her legs and draped them over his shoulders before Tony began sliding his tongue over her hips and pelvic area. In anticipation for what was to happen next, she closed her eyes and felt his tongue traversing her walls and entering inside her. Her stomach tensed up and her eyes and hips began to roll in sync. He then placed his lips around her clit, swollen from the excitement, and began sucking on it softly as his tongue simultaneously moved back and forth gently in and around it. This elicited low pitched moans and deep breaths that caused her back to arch up and her ass to lift off the bed. She began to cry, as she was accustomed to do. Tony knew not to take his eyes off of her, per her past instructions.

As she continued to tense up and roll her hips, she said to him with a pouting tone, "Bae, you eat this pussy so goddamn good!"

Her eyes were wide and starry, as if she had just taken a hit of angel dust, but Tony was her drug of choice.

"You like that, baby?" he asked as he continued licking and sucking her clit, making the smacking sound.

"Yes! And, whatever you do, don't stop! I'm about to cum, Bae!" she pleaded. Her body tensed up more. "Please! Right there!" she exclaimed.

With heavy breathing and body vibrating with ecstasy, she sprayed Tony's face with her hot juices. It looked as if he had just eaten a glazed doughnut. Angela was a squirter. Before, she could finish releasing her load, Tony quickly climbed on top of her and proceeded to go deep inside of her as she shrieked and looked up at the mirrored ceiling directly above the bed. After moments of deep thrusts, she came again and could no longer take anymore. She crawled up backwards towards the head board where she found herself trapped.

She cried out, "Bae! Hold on! Let me catch my breath!" Tony gave her a few seconds, then turned her over onto her knees, face down and ass up. He took his leg and wrapped it around, as if to lock her in. He started thrusting slowly, before applying the pound game on her. With each thrust, she screamed, *"Fuck me, daddy! Fuck this pussy!"* as she looked in the mirror on the head-board. Switching and changing positions, this went on all night. To say that Tony gave her what she wanted was an understatement. He gave her one of the best fucks of her freak bitch life. That Viagra that he popped in his mouth at the restaurant without her knowledge, made that all possible. Not that he needed it, but he needed his dick to stay hard all night.

Early the next morning, Tony was rewarded for last night's performance with his favorite breakfast in bed: Salmon Croquettes, cheese grits, homemade biscuits with country cane syrup, and fresh ground Columbian coffee. Although Angela never lived a day in the south, other than summer visits in Georgia where she first met Tony, she learned how to make southern cuisine from her black father's side of the family. After handing him his breakfast, she kissed him gently on his forehead.

"Good morning, Tony."

"Wow!" he said as he sat up in the bed smiling and stretching with his eyes glued to the plate of food. "A true southern breakfast like Ma used to make. Girl, where you learned to cook like this?" he asked, jokingly.

"Boy, don't even play, you know my father and granny taught me to burn."

"Yeah, I know. And I take it you don't ever want me to go home either, cooking like this." She leaned over and kissed him again.

"Yep! That's the plan, Mr. Stallworth." She sat down beside him.

"Oh yeah, baby. I almost forgot," he said, sipping his coffee. "I've got to catch a flight at six tomorrow morning and I'm gonna need you to shoot me to the airport, if you don't mind."

"Sure, honey, I can get you there," she said with an inquisitive look. Tony quickly began eating his breakfast, hoping she wouldn't ask him where he was going. But to his surprise she didn't. At least not at that time.

Chapter 7

Flight into a New Chapter

Early the next morning Angela scooped up Tony from his crib and drove him to the airport. Nearly the whole way there was silence in the car, except for the song *A Change is Gonna Come* by Sam Cooke playing from the radio. Breaking the silence, Angela placed her hand on Tony's leg. "Tony, I have something to tell you."

"Okay, baby, I'm all ears," he said with his ears pushed forward. The tone of her voice, indicated to him that she was about to say something serious. She looked over at him and saw his antics and laughed.

"You are so silly." She playfully hit him on the arm. "But no seriously, Tony, I have something to tell you."

"Okay, baby, shoot," he said, looking out of his window.

"I was given a job offer in Europe."

"Europe!" he responded with surprise. Her words seemed to catch him off guard. His heart momentarily skipped a beat.

"Yeah, baby, Europe." Tony just sat there not showing any emotions. He didn't want to let on that the news saddened him. "I didn't mention it to you when I first got the offer a couple of weeks ago because I'm not really sure if I should accept the offer." She peered over at Tony to see his facial expression, but there was none.

Pausing momentarily to carefully select his words, he asked, "Well, was it a good offer?" She nodded.

"Yes, it was an extremely good offer, but I didn't know how you would feel about it. I do value your feelings and input, you know."

Tony sat silent, still trying to guard his words and not wanting to come across the wrong way. As she drove, her eyes alternated back and forth between him and the highway as she waited on his response. After a few seconds had passed, and there was no response from Tony, she took the initiative and solicited one. "Well, are you going to comment, Tony?"

He smiled and turned to her. "Baby look. I love you enough to never hinder you or stunt your growth in any way. You're my lover as well as my friend, and I could never hold back a friend from elevating to the next level. If I did that, it would mean that I don't love and care for you as I profess to."

She smiled. Her eyes began to well up with tears. His words seemed to put her at ease and touched her heart at the same time. His initial nonchalant attitude to her news of the job offer concerned her. She had hoped he would show some anguish about her decision. Or maybe even object to it and tell her she wasn't going anywhere. She grabbed his hand.

"I know you care about me," she said. Her voice cracked with emotion. "But I didn't want to take the offer without first discussing it with you and seeing how you felt about it. Besides, I've never been abroad, but once when I was a child. I'm not even sure if I would be happy in a foreign land where I don't know anyone."

"Well, Angela baby, that part of it is entirely up to you. But as far as me objecting to you accepting the job offer and moving towards your goals in life, I'm not going to ever stand in your way, honey."

With that said, for the remainder of the trip nothing else was mentioned on the subject, although the news weighed heavily on both of their minds. Tony was stunned by the news although he didn't show it. It actually hit him like a ton of bricks, but he was the type of cat who never wore his emotions on his sleeve. He knew however, this news of Angela's relocation was the proverbial parting of the ways for their on again, off again relationship. Angela knew it as well. She just continued to look straight ahead with her eyes on the road and her mind on this man sitting next to her that she loved more than anything or anyone in the world. In her mind, all he had to do is say the word and she would reject the job offer without a second thought. But as he stated to her, she knew he would never be the reason why she turned down a chance for career advancement. Tony realized that his lack of emotion to her news may have given her the impression that he could care less, but that wasn't the case at all. Tony really and truly cared deeply for her and would miss her tremendously, but no matter how he felt, he could not keep her from advancing to the next level.

After finally pulling into the airport parking lot, Tony gently clutched her hand and peered into her eyes.

"Baby, look. Please don't think for one moment that I don't care about you leaving and that I won't miss you. Believe me when I say this, baby, that's not the case at all. But like I said to you earlier, I can't and won't hold you back or stand in your way for any reason." Angela smiled and kissed him on the lips.

"I know, baby. I know you love me enough that you would never stand in my way."

It's just the thought of me leaving the country, especially away from you, is a hard pill for me to swallow. That's all. I love you, Tony."

"I love you too, Angela," he said to her as he gently embraced her. After separating from their embrace, Angela wiped her tears away and quickly recovered.

"Tony, baby, if you don't mind me asking, where are you flying to?" Tony smiled.

"Yes, I do mind you asking, nosey!" he said then quickly kissed her on the forehead and climbed out of the car to retrieve his luggage from the trunk. Angela stepped out of the car right in behind him with her hands on her hips.

.ione of my business where you're going?" she
,er neck.

.ıst messing with you, baby," he said laughing with
hıs ₂e in hand. Somewhat relieved, she walked over and
kissea ..m.

"I knew you were only joking with me, baby." He returned
her kiss.

"Yeah, baby, of course I was just joking with you. But you
are kinda nosy though," he said before quickly swinging around
with his luggage and hurrying off to the luggage check-in, laughing his ass off. Angela was able to land a playful parting punch
to his arm before he could make his quick escape.

Smiling, she shook her head and shouted, "Be safe Tony."

Shortly after checking in his luggage, Tony boarded the huge
jumbo jet, sat back in his seat, and attempted to relax, but the old
anxieties of flying began to resurface the moment he had stepped
foot on the plane. Although his soon to be former profession often called for air travel, Tony had always hated flying and this
time was no different. Pondering on what this trip represented,
which was the beginning of a new chapter in his life, somewhat
eased those old anxieties. That was until all the passengers had
boarded the plane and that familiar soft voice came over the P.A.
system.

"Ladies and gentlemen, welcome aboard TWA Luxury Air-
lines." Tony knew this meant that the dreaded takeoff was imminent.

"Please remain seated during takeoff. In the unlikely event of
an emergency, directly above where you are seated are oxygen
masks for your use. And for your convenience, there's a button
to alert our flight attendants in the event you need anything during the flight. Once again, for your safety, please remain in your
seats during takeoff and landing. If there are any questions you

may have, please feel free to ask any of our flight attendants. Thank you for choosing TWA for your air travel."

Moments later the plane's huge engines roared, and shortly thereafter the colossal jumbo jet lifted off from the runway and ascended into the heavens. The two aspects Tony hated most about flying was the takeoff and landing and now that the takeoff was behind him, for now he was finally able to relax enough to fall asleep.

Within a few hours, Tony was awakened by that soft, familiar voice again.

"Ladies and gentlemen, we will be landing in fifteen minutes. The weather in the city of Bogota is sunny with no chance of rain. Once again, thank you for choosing TWA."

Now wide awake upon hearing this, Tony nervously waited for the other part of flying he hated the most, the landing. He figured that the announcement that it would be fifteen minutes before the plane touched the earth would be more like an eternity. However, to his pleasant surprise, it took only nine minutes and forty-five seconds for the plane's tires to come to a screeching halt on the runway with an even more pleasant and smooth landing. This naturally decreased Tony's heart rate back to the normal fifty beats per minute. As the passengers filed out of the plane one by one, Tony sat patiently so he would be the last off the plane. This too was born of habit due to him not liking anyone to be behind him. Whether it was a plane, a bus, or train, it was a sure bet that Tony would be the last person to exit. After the last passenger exited the plane, Tony climbed off and headed straight into the airport to retrieve his luggage. Once he had his luggage in hand, he walked outside and spotted a midget in full chauffeur attire standing beside a black Cadillac limo. The pint-sized man made eye contact with him and motioned with his tiny arms as made his way towards him.

"Senor Stallworth?"

"Si," Tony responded.

"Good to meet you. I am here to take you to Senor Armando's ranchero. Let me take your luggage, sir." Tony was somewhat doubtful that the midget was up for the task. But to his surprise, the midget chauffeur grabbed the luggage and manhandled it with surprising strength, carefully placed it into the trunk of the limo. "Are you ready to go now, Senor Stallworth?"

"Si." The chauffeur strolled to the back passenger door and opened it for Tony before closing it shut. He then walked over to the driver's side, hopped up into the driver's seat, and without any delay they were off to Ranchero Armando. As the limo travelled through the countryside, Tony marveled at the beautiful scenery, which was a mixture of jungle vegetation and the hustle and bustle of Bogota city folk. There were shops, restaurants, fruit and vegetable stands, and peasants on their collective hustles. Even the stray dogs looked as though they were on their hustle, as well, trying to scurry food.

During Tony's past travels, he had visited for both business and personal reasons nearly every nation in North, Central, and South America. He found they all had one thing in common. They were all impoverished nations. Every single one, with the exceptions of America and Canada and for obvious reasons. They are both white nations. Tony, like many revolutionaries, concluded a long time ago that this wasn't a coincidence, but was by design, especially when one takes into consideration the gross domestic product of countries like Columbia which is cocaine. Although illegal, Coke was by far the most valuable, sought after commodity in the western hemisphere, mainly in the U.S. Yet, Columbia is one of the poorest nations on earth. This is how it was the world over. Nations of color being blessed with mineral wealth and the white man is the one becoming wealthy from it, while the indigenous people remain in abject poverty from one generation to the next.

After about twenty minutes into the trek, and now completely surrounded by jungle scenery, the chauffeur ended the tranquility.

"How was your flight, Senor Stallworth?" he asked, alternating his gaze from the interior rearview mirror to the winding dirt road.

"I slept the entire flight, but the landing was rather smooth."

"Well good, good sir. I hope you enjoy your stay here in Bogota as well."

"I certainly plan to," he said, knowing in his mind that he wasn't there for any fun and relaxation, but for business and business only.

"We have less than ten minutes before we reach Senor Armando's helicopter pad."

"Helicopter pad! We've gotta fly?" Tony said, rising up in his seat.

Somewhat startled by Tony's outburst, the driver reluctantly said, "Si Si, Senor Stallworth. Armando's ranchero cannot be accessed by car. Is there something wrong, sir?" Tony smiled.

"No. Everything is alright. I just didn't anticipate on flying twice in one day." The driver peered back at Tony through the mirror and shrugged his tiny shoulders.

"Sorry, Senor Stallworth."

After enduring a somewhat bumpy, but beautifully scenic ride, the limo finally reached the helicopter pad where the chopper and three bodyguards were waiting. Almost immediately, Tony's old anxieties of the dreaded takeoff and landing reared its ugly head. Nevertheless he exited the limo and boarded the chopper without hesitation, while the driver handled his luggage onto the chopper.

"How are you today, sir?" the pilot asked.

"Fine," he responded. *That was until now,* he thought to himself.

"Okay good. We will land at Senor Armando's ranchero in less than fifteen minutes." Tony nodded. *I really hope it's more like five minutes.* Tony really detested flying, but he knew just as he did in past jobs, it all came with the occupation. On many occasions he was contracted to travel great distances to bring a mark's life to an end, but this time was different. Now he was flying a great distance to bring that particular chapter of his life to an end and to begin a new one.

In less than fifteen minutes, just as the pilot had said, Armando's colossal ranch was in sight. Tony was completely awestruck at the size and beauty of it.

"I have never seen anything quite like it," he said to the pilot with amazement. "This is certainly not the ranch I remembered seeing a few years back."

"Si, Senor Stallworth. This is Armando's new ranchero. lt is said to be the biggest in all of Columbia." Tony estimated that Armando's ranch itself was at least the size of ten city blocks, with a huge fortress-like palatial mansion located in the middle of it. Moments later, the chopper touched down as Tony was met by Armando and four men wearing khaki jumpsuits and berets, armed with Uzis. Tony knew they were paramilitary cats. After un-boarding the chopper, Armando greeted Tony with a brisk hug.

"Heeeey, Tony, my friend! How was your trip?"

"Oh it was just fine, Mando. We got here pretty quickly."

"Good, good, my friend. Did you have a chance to eat yet?"

"No sir. I can't say that I have, Mando. And real talk, I can eat a couple of those two pound porterhouse steaks I attempted to eat the last time I was here."

Armando smiled and took a drag from his Cuban cigar. "Well, my friend, Armando's cooks will have a half of a cow prepared for you this time." The two laughed out loud as Armando slapped Tony on his back.

A couple hours later, after dinner the maid cleared the last of the plates and silverware off the table.

"Well, my friend, how was your dinner?" Armando asked.

"Excellent, Mando! Man, I am stuffed." He slumped back in his chair. Armando laughed.

"Any room for dessert?"

"Are you kidding me? I can't eat another bite."

"Good. Good. Glad you enjoyed it," Armando said before taking a deep drag from his cigar. Tony scanned the dining hall which was bigger than most people's entire homes.

"Damn, Mando! This crib is a helluva lot bigger than the one you had in Mexico a few years ago."

Armando laughed. "You like, aye?"

"Like is an understatement! It is absolutely breathtaking!"

"Yes, my friend. I relocated here to Bogota after the death of my Edwina. The seclusion of this place had provided the much needed security for my two children, who are all grown now and are away attending college in Europe."

"Yeah, Mando, you never did find out who was responsible for your wife's murder?" Armando paused momentarily. By the expression on his face, the question seemed to open up old wounds.

"You see, my friend, it was during a war between the cartels when my Edwina was killed. I was the intended target, but unfortunately she died instead of me. So afterwards, a truce was reached, but not before many others died on all sides. This is why I broke away from the politics and bickering of the cartels in Mexico and became independent. But this is the nature of the business we choose to be in."

As Tony sat there, he couldn't help but to think about his own former profession and the business of death that he was all too familiar with.

CATO

Armando puffed on his cigar then said, "My friend, come with me. Let me show you something." He and Tony got up from the table, walked outside, and climbed onto a golf cart, followed by two of Armando's bodyguards in another cart. Within five minutes, they reached a huge factory building with a huge adjacent runway connected to it. Armando and Tony hopped off the cart and walked to the entranceway of the building followed by the stone-faced bodyguards. Armando opened the huge steel doors and revealed inside crates up on crates of kilos of what appeared to be cocaine, marked, compressed, and ready for shipment to perhaps destinations throughout the western hemisphere. After taking a deep drag from his cigar, Armando looked into Tony's eyes.

"This is the stuff dreams are made of, my friend."

"Damn, Mando!" Tony said in amazement. "There's gotta be at least ten thousand keys in here."

Armando chuckled. "Try twenty thousand, my friend. In fact, a shipment of ten thousand just went out two days ago."

"Damn!" Tony said again, as he looked around.

Armando took another puff of his cigar then asked, "What can Armando do for you, my friend?"

"That all depends on the price tag, Mando."

Clutching Tony's shoulder he said, "Price? What kind of friend do you think I am? For you, there is no price up front."

Tony held up his hand in protest. "Now wait a minute, Mando. I have my own bread and I can..."

Armando cut him off.

"No! No, my friend! Keep your money. Armando takes care of the very few friends that he has. And you, Stallworth, you are my friend." Finally Tony relented.

"Okay, Mando," he said smiling. "What do you have in mind?"

58

"Well, how does a thousand keys at eight grand a piece for starters sound?"

"Damn, Mando. I don't know, man. That's a lot of Coke. It may take some time for me to get up off that kinda load, because remember, Mando, this is a whole new market for me."

Armando walked up close to Tony and peered into his eyes. "What has Armando done to receive this kind of treatment? Look around you! Does it look as though Armando is in any dire need of money or anything else for that matter?"

"Okay, Mando. Okay man. You win," he said, smiling.

"Well good! Good, my friend. I knew you would eventually see things Armando's way," he said, hitting Tony on his back.

"Well okay, Mando. Since we are in agreement now, when can we get this show on the road?"

"I can have the first shipment to you as early as one week from today. Does that work for you, my friend?"

"Sure, Mando. That's cool."

"Well okay, it is settled. But you will need a good, secure place to store such a load and future loads."

"No problem. I will be ready when the time comes."

"Very good, my friend. And welcome to the biggest enterprise in the western world." The two men exchanged firm handshakes before heading back to Armando's hacienda, flanked by his killers.

After they made it back inside the huge mansion, Armando poured himself a shot of tequila. "Would you like a drink, my friend?"

"No thank you, Mando."

"Still don't indulge, I see," Armando said smiling before downing his drink. "My friend, Armando has a very small favor to ask of you, if it is at all possible."

"Sure, Mando. What does my good friend need?" Tony said as he sat back in his chair.

"It's just a small thing," Armando said. "There is a fat, greedy, disrespectful bastard in the states. In fact, this individual resides and conducts business right there in your city," he said as he poured himself another shot while Tony listened intently.

"He goes by the name of Ocho Rios. Does this name ring a bell?"

"Can't say that it does. But what do you want done with him?"

Armando fired up a cigar, took a deep drag from it then said in a cold voice, "I want you to bring his disrespectful days to an abrupt and dramatic end. That bastard seems to think it is a game to fuck with Armando's money. But far worse than that, he is now doing business with the very man who I always strongly believed to be responsible for my Edwina's death, my former rival, Domingo Alvarez, with my fucking money."

"Okay. Say no more. Consider it done. Just give me a photo of our disrespectful friend, Mr. Rios, and I'll send him your regards. It would be my pleasure," he said. Although this was the chapter in his life he wanted to close, Tony didn't mind at all doing this favor for this man whom he had mad respect for. An old friend. However, the fact that this favor would further endear him to Mando wasn't lost on him either. Tony knew that in this world, you have to make allies and solidify friendships. And what better close friend and ally to have than the most powerful man in South America?

Armando took another drag from his cigar then let out a huge laugh that echoed off the walls. "I knew you could help Armando fix this little problem!" After a few more minutes of small talk, exhausted and drained from jet lag, Tony decided to turn it in for tonight.

"Well, Mando, I'm going to retire for the evening so I can get some rest. I'll be leaving early for the states first thing tomorrow morning."

"So soon, my friend? I thought you were taking a vacation?"

"Vacation? Man, with all this work ahead of me, I'll need to get back and get busy right away."

"I understand," Armando said as he and Tony stood up and shook hands. "Business is first. And this is the key to achieving success in any business. You get rich first, then your rest." Tony smiled.

"That's exactly the plan I'm going to follow, Mando." With that said, Tony retired for the evening.

Early the next morning, Tony said goodbye to Armando before the pilot flew him back to the airport where he later caught an 8 a.m. flight back to the crib. Hours later he arrived at JFK where Genie was waiting out in the airport parking lot.

"What it do, Genie?" Tony said after hopping in Genie's ride.

"Oh not a whole lot. Slow motion actually. So how was your trip, bruh?"

"Very rewarding, Genie Boy. Very rewarding." Genie alternated looks between Tony and the road as he made his way out of the airport and onto the highway.

"That's what's up, bruh. But what was so very rewarding, T? Tell me something good, kid?"

"Everythang Gucci." Genie looked over at him again as he continued to maneuver the vehicle.

"Okay, well I'm listening." Tony peered out of his window and smiled.

"Genie, you recall our little conversation a few days ago about us getting off into something more profitable and with less hands-on involvement?"

"Yeah, I remember."

"Well, my brother, that time is at hand. I just hollered at a man who is about to put it in our lives."

"Okay, T, I'm listening," Genie said anxiously.

"Bruh, we're going into the import business."

"The import business? Importing what?" Genie asked with a confused look on his face. Tony looked over at him with a wide smile.

"We are going to be getting an import which happens to be the best gross domestic product of the nation of Columbia. Straight from the jungles of Bogota, Columbia to be exact."

"You talking Coke, T?"

"Already, nigga! For the best price, the best quality, with shipping and handling free of charge. I'm talking fish scale type shit."

"Okay. So when is this man gone put it in our lives?"

"Real soon, Genie. But in the meantime, bruh, we have one last loose end to take care of as a favor to this man." Passing Genie the picture of Ocho Rios, Tony parroted Armando's word. "It's just a small thing."

Genie analyzed the photo carefully. "Does that cat look familiar to you, Genie?" Genie nodded his head as the familiarity of the man in the photo began to register in his mind.

"Damn, T! Yeah, I know this cat here from somewhere. Or at least I've seen him before somewhere." As he continued to drive, Genie was searching the files in his memory banks to I.D. the fat man in the photo.

Ending the suspense, Tony asked, "Does the name Ocho Rios ring a bell?"

Almost as soon as he said it, "Yeah! Yeah!" Genie blurted out as he swerved over into the other lane of traffic, nearly causing an accident. "Yeah, T, this is the Columbian cat who be supplying that triple O.G. Natty Boy and the other niggas over on the east side."

"Well, they'll need to find them another plug like real soon."

"T, man, this cat Ocho is a pretty heavy dude with some pretty heavy security around him at all times." Tony nodded and smiled.

"Yeah, Genie. I can see in the photo he's heavy, and I plan to take some of that weight off his ass." Genie chuckled. Tony then turned to him with a deadly serious look on his face.

"Genie, you've known me long enough to know better than anyone that when I got business on a mark, his ass got problems. No matter what kinda bodyguards or security he's got, I don't see none of that shit. In fact, Genie, if I had business on the fuckin' President of the United States, Barack Obama, with all his body-guards and Secret Service, they couldn't and wouldn't prevent me from getting to his ass, you feel me? Now they may in fact get me in the process, but not before I take a few of them with me and bring his presidency to an untimely end." Genie smiled and nodded his head in agreement.

"I know, T, cause yousa baaad man!" They both laughed and gave each other dap. "So okay, bruh, when do we pay ole fat boy a visit?"

"You know the routine, my nigga. Soon after I do my usual homework to peep out his movements. But in the meantime, Genie, I need you to secure a sizable place to store the load. Preferably a storage."

"Okay T, I have just the place in mind."

"I also need you to round up a crew of about ten stand-up cats and have them meet us at the Savoy bar at six sharp tomorrow night."

Later that evening, after getting some much needed rest, Tony called Angela. Since he'd gotten back, she had constantly been on his mind after she gave him the news about her job offer in Europe. After about eight rings, and no answer, he got her voicemail. "Hello, you've reached Angela Washington. Sorry that I'm not in right now, but please feel free to leave a message."

"Hey, babygirl, what's up? Just trying to get at you to let you know I made it back to the crib. I'll holla back at you later, baby."

After placing the phone down on the hook, he began staring at the photo of Ocho he held in the other hand.

"Well, Mr. Rios, it looks like I'll be looking in on your ass tonight," he said as he laid the photo down on his dresser before walking to the closet. After slipping into all black, he went to the safe that contained some of the deadly tools of his trade, which consisted of night vision binoculars, a ski mask, a survival vest with inserts that housed a combat knife, two steel throwing balls, and six small throwing knives. He then reached into a metal box inside the safe, and grabbed a .22 caliber pistol and a silencer.

After gathering all the other tools he needed for the surveillance of Ocho, he grabbed a change of clothes, neatly placed them into a black leather tote bag, turned on some music, and chilled in his recliner in complete darkness to await nightfall. *As No More Pain* by 2Pac blared throughout the room, the cell phone rang, but Tony didn't move a muscle. He just sat there silent as if he was in some sort of hypnotic trance. His face was icy cold. He was as poised as a predator lying in wait for its prey. Finally, at the onset of nightfall, Tony rose up from the chair, grabbed the tote bag that contained his deadly tools, and then darted out of into the night like a vampire in search of a hapless victim.

Chapter 8

The Hit on Ocho Rios - Tony's Last Hit

After about a half hour of driving, Tony finally spotted Ocho's huge crib over in Brooklyn Heights. After circling the block a couple times to check out the layout of the area and seeing that all was clear, Tony parked a couple of blocks away from Ocho's crib, cut his engine and lights, and began peering intently at the huge mansion through his night vision binoculars. Scanning the mansions perimeter, he immediately noticed two of Ocho's bodyguards standing on the south side end of the mansion having a conversation. On the far end, he noticed four more sitting in a pavilion engaged in a friendly game of cards.

From his observations and vantage point, there were a total of six men occupying the front of the crib, there were no signs of any additional men. Moments later, he spotted some movement in an upstairs bedroom, but couldn't make out who it was before the person quickly disappeared from sight. Then suddenly, the mystery person reappeared on the bedroom's balcony laughing aloud and talking into the phone. It was fat boy, Ocho Rios, all 350 pounds of him. As Tony's eyes locked on him through his night vision binoculars, he thought to himself, *Damn! If I had brought along my Rem 700 I could go ahead and take care of ole fat boy right now.* But fortunately for Ocho, this was just homework for Tony, at least that was the plan. A few minutes later, Ocho left the balcony and walked back into the interior of the bedroom as he continued to talk on the phone before disappearing from view.

Tony laid the binoculars down on the seat to take a short break and looked at his watch. It was five 'til eight. After a short recess from class, he resumed his surveillance of fat boy just in time to see Ocho's garage door peel open, and his men scramble to their feet trying to appear busy guarding their boss' life. Seconds later, Ocho's driver emerged from his living quarters located behind the house, climbed into the driver's seat of a pearl white Bentley, and fired up the engine while Tony sat patiently in stealth, with his eyes fixed on this fast developing situation.

Where are you headed, fat boy? he thought to himself as he peered intently through the binoculars. *I know your ass is going somewhere because if not, why would your driver walk out of his living quarters in full uniform, crank up your ride and just sit there waiting?* Moments later, when Tony spotted Ocho exiting the front door he answered his own question. *I know why, Ocho! Because you are on your way somewhere. And it appears like you're only taking one of your so-called bodyguards along with you. And it also appears Mr. Rios that you've just fucked up.*

Tony's calculations were right. Ocho's Bentley backed out of the garage and out of the long stone driveway. As the pearl white Bentley approached his position, Tony slid further down in the seat to avoid detection. Giving Ocho a few seconds to pass, Tony rose back up in his seat and quickly looked back in the direction of the mansion to make sure none of Ocho's men were following him. As soon as their boss was out of sight, they were all back in the pavilion resuming their friendly game of cards. *Good help sure is hard to find these days,* Tony thought to himself as he calmly placed his binoculars down on the seat. After counting to ten, he cranked up his ride and began methodically tracking Ocho like a prairie wolf.

Once Ocho's Bentley was about four blocks ahead of him heading west, Tony turned on his lights and continued to hang in behind them. As he continued his steady pursuit, he reached into the glove compartment and grabbed his throwaway cell phone and placed a call to Genie.

"Genie in the bottle! Genie in the bottle! Come in Genie!"

Seconds later, "Genie here. What's up, T?"

Gangsta Shyt

"You mean what's going down, Genie!" Genie paused momentarily not exactly sure as to what his partner was talking about.
"That little business with fat boy, my brother," Tony said.
"Oh, real talk, T?"
"Real talk, bruh," Tony said with a wicked grin on his face. "And he's headed west on Beaver St. as we speak."
"Where do you think our friend is headed, T?"
"This time of the night, Genie, I'm willing to bet his fat ass done got hungry and is on his way to get something to eat. But peep this shit, bruh. Our little fat friend has only one lone body-guard accompanying him to retrieve his late night snack."
"Only one bodyguard!" Genie said in total disbelief.
"Yep! Just one, my brother. But you know what, Genie? If my instincts are correct, I believe he's headed to that steakhouse on Beaver Street. What is it called?"
"You talking about that steak joint, Delmonico?"
"Sho' you right!" Tony exclaimed with sinister delight. "Delmonico, where all the mobsters and big timers hang out. Okay, Genie, where are you at right now, my brother?"
"I'm less than a mile from Beaver Street."
"Okay cool. I want you to post up in the parking lot of the Hilton that sits kitty-corner to the steak house and wait there for me."
"Okay, T. Roger that. I'm on my way."
"Oh yeah, Genie, before you sign off, did you just so happen to bring that tool with you?"
"You already know. I keep that on deck," he said.
"Okay, that's what's up. Bet. At you in a minute." Just as Tony had called it, Ocho's Bentley turned south on Beaver St. in the direction of Delmonico Steakhouse as Tony quickly closed in behind them. Once at the light, Tony hit Genie back. "Alright,

bruh. That package is en route and should be coming your way. Are you in position?"

"Yeah, T, I'm here posted up in the cut. And as you called it, our friend's pearl white Bentley with the gangster white walls just pulled up to the Steakhouse. T, yousa baaaaad man!"

"And you know it!" Tony exclaimed. "Okay, Genie, stay put and I'll be there in a sec."

A couple of minutes later, Tony swung into the parking lot of the Hilton where his partner was backed in with his eyes trained on the Steakhouse. After pulling in behind him, and cutting his engine, Tony hopped into Genie's back seat donning a hungry croc grin on his face.

"Is our friend inside, Genie?"

"Yeah, his fat ass is in there with his bodyguard…probably eating up every damn thang on the menu." Tony peered across the street as he screwed the silencer to his .22 caliber pistol.

"You know I really hadn't planned on finishing this business with Mr. Rios so soon," Tony said with his eyes still locked onto the restaurant. "I was only doing a little homework on him when this fool slipped and left his crew at the crib." Genie stared at the Steakhouse and shook his head in total disbelief.

"I can't believe this fool only got one bodyguard with him knowing his fat ass is delinquent on somebody's funds. Unbelievable!"

"Yeah, but not just somebody's money, Genie. He fucked over one of the most powerful, most wealthy, and most dangerous men in all of South America." Genie peered into the mirror at Tony and grinned devilishly.

"And now he's got the most dangerous man in North America waiting outside for his ass." The two chuckled and gave each other dap.

"Okay Genie." Tony locked his eyes on to the front entrance of the restaurant. "Here's the plan. When Ocho's driver swings around in front of the restaurant, and the bodyguard comes out ahead of Ocho to secure the area, I want you to drive in his direction real slow, lay into the horn as soon as you get in front of the restaurant then hit the gas and floored it out of there. This will cause a distraction. Afterwards, meet me at the Savoy bar. I'll be there shortly thereafter."

After about an hour and a half had passed, Ocho's Bentley finally pulled around in front of the restaurant.

"Okay, T, we've got movement." Tony rose up in the seat.

"Okay, Genie, let's do this shit," Tony said before Genie fired up his ride and slowly headed onto Beaver Street. When Genie slowed down to a crawl, Tony hopped out with the Mac 11 machine gun pistol in his hand that he had inquired about earlier and crouched down behind one of several parked cars lined up on the curb. While Genie crept onward towards the front entrance of the restaurant, Tony pulled the black ski mask down over his head and remained out of sight with the Mac 11 clutched in his hand.

Just as Genie was about to pass in front of the steak house, the bodyguard walked out onto the sidewalk and scanned the area, looking from side to side as if his head was a rotating fan. When Genie got directly in front of the restaurant, he laid into the horn just as Tony had instructed him to, then floored it away from the scene with tires screeching and rubber burning.

Somewhat startled by the commotion, the bodyguard took a step back, ran his hand inside his suit jacket and placed it on his heater with his eyes glued in the direction Genie traveled. He then cautiously stepped out a little further from the curb to further assess the threat. Once he figured the errant vehicle was gone and there was no danger, he motioned for Ocho to come out. Following his bodyguard's instructions, Ocho proceeded to walk out slowly, laughing and talking loud with the restaurant manager as if he didn't have a care in the world. He was totally oblivious to the fact that death was waiting on his ass just a few feet away.

Meanwhile, Tony remained crouched down behind a tour bus cradling his tool in his arms with his eyes locked on Ocho's partially visible body, patiently waiting for the right moment to pounce. When Ocho's huge overlapping stomach began to appear past the corner of the building, and the restaurant manager turned and started heading back inside the restaurant, Tony began his low death trot toward Ocho like a hungry lion on the Serengeti creeping up on its prey. As soon as Ocho's fat frame finally came into full view, Tony suddenly popped up in front of him and his unsuspecting bodyguard so fast it looked like a blur, and sprayed them with a deadly hail of nine millimeter brass from the Mac 11.

Those poor bastards never knew what hit'em. The awful sound of the Mac spittin' round after deadly round, fifty rounds per second, was the last thing Ocho and his bodyguard heard. The Mac's deafening rapid fire explosion was enough to scare off any nosey ass, would-be eye witnesses. As the two men laid there sprawled with their bodies kicking in a death spasm, Tony calmly took out his .22 caliber and finished the business with Ocho by giving him two shots to the dome. By this time, Ocho's driver had hit three parked cars fleeing the scene, perhaps thinking his ass was next. Tony then calmly turned around and trotted back to his ride, cranked it, and calmly drove away from the scene, hitting block after block as the approaching sirens echoed in the distance. Ocho and his bodyguard's lifeless, bullet riddled corpses laid stretched out in front of the restaurant's flower bed in a pool of blood with their eyes wide open and a look of shock and horror entombed on their faces.

After a quick change of clothes and switching vehicles a short time later, Tony pulled into the Savoy parking lot. When he walked inside, he spotted Genie standing at the bar downing a drink. Tony strolled up behind him and whispered in his ear, "Imma baaaaaaaaaaad man!"

Genie slowly turned around to face him with the empty shot glass in his hand and said, "Already." After ordering another shot of Crown, Genie mentioned to Tony about the building he secured for the load and the cats he recruited.

When the ten o'clock news popped on the big screen above the bar, Genie nudged Tony and motioned to it. The bartender killed the volume on the jukebox, turned up the volume on the T.V., then motioned for the Savoy's few patrons to be quiet.

"Good evening, I'm Lisa Carlton, here on the scene in front of Delmonico's Steakhouse on Beaver Street, a popular dining spot for the Brooklyn Heights' elite. What happened here tonight, just a little over an hour ago was a blazoned and dramatic attack reminiscent of a scene right out a gangland movie. According to shaken eyewitnesses, reputed Colombian drug kingpin, Ocho Rios, and his bodyguard were cut down in a hail of gunfire shortly after eating dinner inside the restaurant. One frightened eyewitness, who asked not to be identified, said that it was as if a phantom suddenly appeared out of the night, did the deed, and disappeared back into the darkness."

Genie grinned and whispered to Tony, "You *are* a bad man."

The Savoy's patrons, along with the bartender, immediately began gossiping and speculating among themselves as to who was behind the hit, and the many reasons behind it. After a few more minutes of being amused by the patrons' conspiracy theories, better known as CPN, or Colored Peoples News, Genie downed his third and final drink.

"Hey T, I'm about to take it in, kid. What you got going tonight?"

"I think I'll sit here for a while longer and chill out for a little while. I had planned to take Angela out tonight, but she was tied up with her job earlier." Genie smiled.

"T, man when you gonna go ahead on and give that woman what she been wanting for a long time?" Tony knew he was talking about the M-word.

"Now Genie, you are my nigga. Of all people, you know better than anyone that I can't stain that broad with my dirt."

"Well, T, that was before your retirement, which officially began about a couple hours ago. And you know the woman is a good catch for you, especially since you're opening up this new chapter in your life and all."

"Yeah, Genie, I know she's a good catch for me. I can't deny that one. But she accepted a job offer in Europe or somewhere, and that's that."

"She accepted a job in *Europe*?" Genie asked in surprise.

"Yep. In Europe," Tony said in a dejected voice.

"Wow!" Genie said shaking his head. "Now that's some real sad shit there. The one good catch that got away. All these thots out here and you let that broad get away? Bruh, you need to lock her in. It ain't like you getting any younger."

"Genie, I feel you on that, bruh. But I just can't hold her back no matter how much I'm feeling her."

"Yeah I hear you, T," Genie said, shaking his head as he paid his tab. "Okay, T, I'll tell those cats to be at the meeting place at six sharp. See you then."

"Alright later, Genie." Tony thought about what Genie said about Angela. He was right. She was wifey material. However, he wasn't husband material. At least not at this time.

Chapter 9
A Second Chance Encounter

As the music bounced off the walls of the Savoy club, people started to trickle in one by one, then two by two, until the club swelled into a nice crowd. The club's DJ started doing his thing at eleven o'clock. He played an array of old school rap and the up to date shit that echoed off the walls of the club. Tony sat in the very back of the Savoy with his back to the wall chilling, sipping on club soda, and listening to the music. A few minutes later, three broads walked in just as Tony was making his way to the bar to grab another soda.

"Hey y'all, I can sure use a drink right about now," one of the broads said.

"Yeah, I can use one too, gurl," the other one said. "Bartender, can you get me a Grey Goose and cranberry, please? And what y'all want, gurl?"

"I'll have some Patron," said Brenda, the other heavy set one. The third broad, a Coke bottle shaped, pecan tan skinned dime wearing long African braids, classy and reserved, unlike her two road dogs, said in a soft but confident voice, "I'll take a Hennessy and Coke on the rocks, please."

While Tony stood there sipping on his soda and listening to the music and not really paying them any attention, the two loud broads started looking over at him, whispering and giggling like two adolescent girls.

"Guuurl, look at that fine ass nigga *right there!*"

"Yeah I see him, gurl, standing over there acting like he don't see us. He must be one of them stuck up ass niggas." The fine, classy one, who acted as though she didn't know the other two ghetto broads, just stood off to herself taking short sips of her drink, and casually moving her well put together frame to the beat of Blurred Lines by Pharrell and Robin Thicke.

"Hey, Sugar. Guuuurl, come check out this fine ass nigga standing over here at the bar," Wanda said. Taking her time, Sugar nonchalantly turned around with her drink in her hand, still bopping her head to the rhythm of the music.

"Ummm hmmm," she said, then immediately turned away without missing a beat. She was totally disinterested in what they were talking about, and stuck in her own little world. A man was the last thing she was interested in, unlike her thirsty road dogs.

Also pre-occupied in his own little world, Tony placed his empty glass down on the bar, leaned over and said to the broads, "It isn't nice to whisper, ladies," he said to them playfully.

After being cold busted, the two hood rats looked at each other in surprise and burst into ghettofied laughter with their drinks sloshing back and forth in their hands. Still moving to the beat, Sugar turned around slowly to see what the commotion was about. When her eyes shifted to the tall, light-skinned, green-eyed cat with mannequin like features, she immediately let out a deep gasp, nearly spilling what was left of her drink which caught Tony's attention. She looked as if she saw a ghost. Or a killer.

"You alright, little mama?" he asked with concern.

"Yeah, yeah, I'm fine," she said as she gathered herself. Tony analyzed her momentarily.

"Are you sure you alright?" he asked, gently touching her arm.

She jerked her arm away from his gentle grip and responded with hostility, "*Look!* I said I was fine, alright!"

"Okay, little mama." he said, pulling his hands back in a defensive posture. "I didn't mean any harm."

"Hey, I'm *not* yo mama. *Okay!*" she shot back.

"I know you're not my mother, she was a helluva lot nicer than you," he said before retreating back to his table.

"Well *good for you, nigga!*" she said defiantly.

74

"Damn, Sugar! Why you tripped on the man like that?" Brenda said. "He was just trying to be nice."

"Guuurl, you must know that nigga or sumpin.'" Wanda said with a chuckle.

"No, Wanda, I don't know him, and never even seen him before." Brenda laughed and nudged Wanda.

"Gurl, are you suuuure you never been acquainted with that fine ass nigga before?" she asked, winking her eye. The two broads then started laughing and falling all over each other again, and spilling the contents of their glasses. It was obvious to everyone that they couldn't handle their liquor. Sugar rolled her eyes with indignation and sighed deeply.

"You know what? Y'all really are some silly-ass bitches! I done told y'all I don't know that nigga!"

They looked at each other and said at the same time, "Whatever bitch!" Again, they broke out into laughter, but even louder this time, steadily falling on each other. Sugar rolled her eyes and sucked her teeth and tore out to the edge of the dance floor. Almost immediately, some cat with dreads, who'd had his eyes glued on her the moment she walked in, intercepted her and began sweating her for a dance, and she reluctantly accepted. They made their way to the semi-crowded dance floor. As they danced, the lower half of Sugar's body began to slowly gyrate in hypnotic and seductive movements to the beat of music, sending every cat in the club into a deep, mind-numbing trance, including Tony, who was pretending to be unmoved. Like the other cats, he could not help but to take notice of how bad this broad was. She wasn't a dime. She was a fifty cent piece. The skirt she wore, did the perfectly proportioned contours of her body justice. Something else Tony took notice of was that this broad never broke her gaze on him the entire time she was on the dance floor.

The thought then hit him, *That face. That body. Where have I seen this broad at before? I know I've seen her somewhere not long ago, but where? I can't place her. I believe she's seen me too, because of her reaction when she saw me and the way she's been staring at me.*

After the song ended, her lame ass dance partner tried to secure another dance with her, but she promptly declined him. When that failed, he attempted get the digits, but before he could ask, she boned out on his ass and retreated across the dance floor in Tony's direction with her eyes fixated on him. Seeing her coming directly at him, he thought to himself, *Oh fuck! This bitch must be crazy or something. I sure hope she ain't coming over here to clown on a nigga again.*

"Hey I..."

"Hey, look lady!" Tony said, cutting her off. "Before you start tripping, I don't want any drama. I'm just out here to chill and listen to some music. Okay?"

"No, you look nigga! I was just coming over here to apologize to you! So I apologized, now *good night!* "

Before she could turn and walk away, Tony stood up and grabbed her arm gently. "Wait a minute, baby. Don't leave. I thought you were coming over here to clown on me. I apologize, and I accept yours," he said as she stood there with her hands on her curvy hips and a look of apprehension on her face.

"Well, you thought wrong," she said defiantly.

Tony held up his hands in surrender. "Okay, Miss Lady, okay," he said extending his hand in peace. "I'm Tony." She looked down at this hand and reluctantly shook it.

"Would you please have a seat for a minute?" Tony said, pulling out a chair. "What is your name?"

"Yeah, I guess I can for a minute," she said with a cautious look. "My name is Sugar." She sat down and scanned the club. "Hey man, you don't have some jealous girl in here do you? Because I'm from the projects, and I *will* cut a bitch." Tony laughed and shook his head.

"No, Sugar, I don't have anyone in here, so you don't have anything to worry about."

"Oh I *know* I don't have shit to worry about, but a bitch coming over here with sumpin' on her mind, she will have plenty to worry about," she said, taking her hand out of her purse." Her face was deadly serious. Tony laughed.

"You're good, baby. I put that on everything. So Sugar, can I get you a drink or something?"

"Nah, no thank you, I'm good."

After gazing at her for a few seconds, and trying not to look star struck he said, "You know, you look so familiar to me. In fact, I swear I've seen you somewhere before."

"Well, maybe you have."

"Where?" he asked.

"Okay, I'll give you a small hint. Early one morning outside of a certain after-hours joint." Immediately, the smile on his face dropped a notch, but not enough for her to notice it. There was no need for her to go any further. He automatically knew exactly when, where, and what she was hinting at.

I knew I saw her somewhere before, he thought to himself.

"Okay, you were the young lady wearing the braids standing on the sidewalk away from the crowd, right?" Sugar smiled and nodded her head. But almost immediately, Tony's mind began to race as it dawned on him that this broad could place him at the scene of Kansas City's murder. "Well Sugar, did you happen to see what went on out there that night?" he asked as he sipped his club soda. His body language and facial expressions were guarded.

"Nah, I was inside the club. And no I could care less about what happened that night or who had something to do with it," she stated matter-of-factly. Tony stared at her momentarily.

"It didn't bother you that a man died out there that night?" he asked.

"No. Not *that* man," she shot back. "I hated that bastard. He was a cruel, grimey ass pimp who finally got what he deserved. He disfigured a girl's face I know."

Tony was somewhat at ease now, but he continued to monitor her eyes and body language for any signs of deceit. "You know, Sugar, hatred is a very heavy burden to carry around on your shoulders. I made it a policy a long time ago to never become so involved in my feelings about anyone or anything enough to hate. In other words, I look at most people and situations as business, never personal. Just business."

"Well, Mr. Tony, I'm not that disciplined with my feelings. Sorry," she said, shrugging her shoulders.

"Sugar, you should try practicing that sometimes, because channeling and limiting your emotions is very liberating." With one last question on his mind he asked, "Sugar, your friends over there, did you share with them about our little chance encounter that night outside the club?"

Realizing the nature of his question, she smiled. "Look man! You can just rest your nerves, okay? Like I said, I didn't see anything that night. And no I didn't tell them about our little chance encounter. Besides, they aren't really my friends anyway. I just came out with them."

Now completely at ease, he smiled and leaned back in his chair. "Okay. We good then," he said smiling. They both chuckled, letting their collective guards down at this point.

"Sugar, would you like to dance?"

"Sure. But you better behave yourself. I told you I'm from the projects, and I don't mind cutting.'" They both laughed before they got up from the table and headed onto the dance floor. While they danced, Sugar's two buddies rolled their eyes with utter jealousy.

"Brenda, look at that bitch," Wanda said.

"Yeah, she always did think she was better than us."

Tony saw the hatred in their eyes. "Your two road dogs over there don't look too happy right now." He smiled.

"Yeah, I see those hating ass bitches over there. Now you see what I meant when I said they're not my friends? But they'll be alright though." She chuckled. After dancing to their third and final song, *All Eyes On You* by Chris Brown, Meek Mill Ft. Nikki Minaj, they returned to the table.

"Sugar, you moved pretty well out there on the dance floor. Like one of those broads on a rap video."

"Well, you don't move bad at all yourself, Tony."

"I've been known to cut a step or two in my day." He smiled at her. "Sugar, what is your real name, if you don't mind me asking?"

"Maybe I do mind you asking. What is your real name?" Tony chuckled.

"You should never answer a question with a question, Sugar."

"And who made that rule?"

"Well I did. It's called the Tony Stallworth rule." She laughed.

"Ohhh okaaay. So your last name is Stallworth, huh?"

"Damn!" He laughed. "I done slipped and gave up the last name first."

"Yeah, you did." She laughed again.

"Okay, now that you know my name, what is yours, babygirl? Your *real* name?"

"Okay, Mr. Stallworth. I guess I can tell you now that I had my question answered first. My name is Constance Jones."

"Hmmm, Constance Jones, huh? Has a nice ring to it. It ain't an alias is it?

"No. It's my real name." She smiled at him.

"Okay. I believe you. Well, I have another question."

"Alright. Let's have it."

"Where did the name Sugar come from?"

"You just had to ask that." She laughed, shaking her head as she thought back to where the nickname matriculated.

"Yep. You already know. I wanna know everything that there is to know about you. So let's have it. How did they come up with Sugar?"

"When I was a kid, I used to sneak into the sugar jar and eat sugar, hence the nickname, Sugar."

"You ate raw sugar?"

"Yes. I ate raw sugar. I loved that stuff."

"So you were a little sugar bandit. I have to say it doesn't show on you now."

"I was a three sport athlete, so I burned most of it off."

"Well, I have my own little confession to make. When I was a shorty I had a sweet tooth also. I had a fondness for cakes and cookies, but now I try to stay away from sugar of any kind."

"Oh yeah? Well, not me. I just had some cheesecake from Junior's yesterday and it was *like that*, I must say." Tony laughed.

"A trip to Junior's is excusable," he said with a chuckle. "Wait a minute. Did you say you were a three sport athlete, Sugar?"

"Yes I did. I played volleyball, track and basketball."

"Wow! So you were a serious athlete, then."

"Yes. Serious enough that it took me on a full ride scholarship to Columbia University."

"Hmmmm. That explains the figure," he quipped.

"Huh?" she asked with a confused look.

"Oh, I mean your build. It's athletic," he replied as Sugar looked at him sideways. "Ummm, what I mean is, you are fine as fuck, baby."

"Thank you." She smiled slightly. Sugar had heard a million times in her adult life how fine she was.

"I'm sure you get that all the time from dudes and broads."

"Yeah I do get that from dudes. The last broad who tried me like that, I hit her over the head with a beer bottle."

"Damn!" Tony said. "Those stud bitches are bold nowadays."

"Yeah. And I'm crazy as fuck and don't play about shit like that."

"I feel ya on that, little mama," he said laughing. "So where are you originally from, Sugar? With that accent, I know you're not a native New Yorker."

"No, I'm not a native New Yorker, and thank God. I'm a native Floridian. I'm from Orlando."

"Oh okay. That's what's up. The sunshine state? I have folks on my old girl's side in Tallahassee and Panama City."

Sugar nodded her head. "I used to hang out down on Panama City Beach for spring break. You got me missing home talking about Florida."

"My bad. When was the last time you went to the crib?"

"It's been about a year now since I last went home."

"Now you know that's not good, little mama. You should get home to your people more often."

"Yeah, well I plan to very soon. I really miss being home, and above all, I miss my granny," she said with an endearing look on her face.

"Well, grannies are special. I lost both of mine when I was a shorty."

"I'm sorry to hear that, Tony."

"Don't be. It's okay. They were both rather old and lived long, prosperous lives. It was just their time. There's nothing wrong with dying if you handle all your affairs and fulfilled all your dreams while on earth."

"Yeah I guess you're right. But that is a pretty unemotional way to look at it."

"Well, I'm a person who's used to death. When I was in Afghanistan, I saw some situations where death could sometimes be our best friend."

"Hmmm. Okay. Now that is pretty deep, in fact too deep for me, sir." Tony laughed.

"I completely understand, Sugar. Death is something most people try not to think about," he said before quickly changing the subject. "Sugar, what are you doing tomorrow night?"

"Nothing at this time. At least I don't have anything planned."

"Okay, good. I will pick you up around 7."

"Wait! Hold on a minute, Mr. Stallworth. I said I didn't have anything planned. That didn't mean I agreed to go out with you."

"And why is that, little mama?"

"Why is what, Mr. Stallworth?"

"Why haven't you agreed to go out with me, yet?"

"Maybe because you never asked." Tony laughed.

"Okay, Ms. Jones. You got me there. Now, will you go to dinner with me tomorrow night?"

"Mmmm, let me see. Since you asked this time instead of telling me, yeah I guess so, Mr. Stallworth. But instead of 7 as you *insisted* instead of asking, we will change that and say 7:30, how about that?" Before he could answer she answered for him, "Yeah, okay. 7:30 sounds better."

"Okay, Ms. Jones, I get your drift. I see you are a strong minded, independent black woman. So it's a mistake for a cat to dictate to you," he said smiling. Tony really admired her feistiness.

"Oh we cool. Just as long as you don't forget that from here on out, sir."

"Trust me. I won't ever make that mistake again, Ms. Jones."

"Okay. We good then." She smiled again. "Well, Tony, I really enjoyed our conversation tonight, but I think I better get back over there before my so-called friends leave my black ass here." "Likewise, Sugar. I am fortunate to have this second chance encounter with you tonight." He stood up and grasped her hand. "Hey! I don't have a contact number or an address to pick you up at."

"That's because you didn't ask for that either, Mr. Stallworth. You need to tighten up your game a little. Hit me up on Facebook. I'm under Constance Jones."

"Facebook? I don't do Facebook, babygirl," he said with a wrinkle on his face. "I'm a little old school when it comes to shit like that."

"Okay. I hear you. You better get with the 21st century then, sir."

"Well, I guess I won't ever upgrade, because that Facebook shit is a fed trap."

"Okay. I feel ya on that. Let me get your number," she said as she took out her iPhone.

"718-521...."

"Okay. I will hit you tomorrow," she said before heading back over to join her two frienemies. She gave all eyes trained on her something to look at. *I kinda dig this broad,* Tony smiled and thought to himself. As she walked away, she smiled and thought to herself, *damn that nigga is fine!*

CATO

Chapter 10
An Organization Is Born

Early the next morning, after performing his usual workout ritual, Tony met up with Angela for lunch at Keen's Steak House. Afterwards, he chilled out at the crib until four o'clock. At a quarter 'til five, one hour prior to the meeting, he was sitting inside the Savoy talking with its owner, triple O.G. Stax, as he waited for Genie and the fresh recruits to show up. At a quarter 'til six, Genie walked in.

"What up, T? What up, Stax?"

"Oh it ain't nothing, Genie," Tony and Stax said.

"Those cats should be here any minute now." Genie ordered a drink from the waitress.

"I sure hope so, Genie," Tony said, looking at his watch. "You know how big I am on punctuality."

"Yeah I know, bruh, and that's why I told them to make sure they be on point," Genie said before he and Tony walked to the back of the club and sat down at a long table with their backs facing the wall. Tony took a look at his watch again. "Genie, man, these cats better be on their way here, because it's already five 'til six and I have a very serious date tonight with a very bad broad."

"Who? Angela?" Tony smiled and shook his head no. "No not Angela?" Genie said. Again Tony shook his head no.

"Well, if not Angela, then who, kid?" Tony gave Genie a firm pat on his shoulder and smiled.

"I'll fill you in on that later, Genie boy. But in the meantime, where are these niggas at you recruited?" he asked again peering at his watch.

"I don't know," Genie replied before heading to the door to see if he could spot them. As soon as Genie reached the door, he was met by six of the recruits. Coming in right behind them was the remaining four as Genie looked at his watch frowning.

"Professor, man, where the fuck have y'all been? I told you my man don't dig tardiness."

"I know, and my bad, Genie, but I had to give some of these cats a ride. My apologies again man." The others followed suit by extending their apologies also.

A voice then said, "Don't be sorry, just be on point the next time I call a meeting. That's *if* you want to be in this shit with us."

The men maneuvered around to get a glimpse of the man that imposing voice came from.

"That's my man, Tony," Genie said. "Y'all niggas come on over here and catch a seat."

Following his orders, the recruits all strolled over to the back of the Savoy where Tony was sitting, and sat down at the table. Tony analyzed each of them for a few seconds with a serious look on his face before addressing them.

"As you just saw, gentlemen, I'm very big on punctuality," he said, standing to his feet. "And like I stressed a minute ago, if you want to be a part of this organization, you be on point when you are summoned, you feel me?" Everyone nodded their heads. "Okay, I want all of you to tell me your names, starting with you on my left."

"I'm the Professor," the older distinguished looking cat wearing glasses said.

"I'm Sandman."

"Chi-Town."

"Black."

"Lil' Larry."

"G."

"Tripp."

"Memphis."

"King."

"Macky Boy."

"Okay. I'm Tony. My partner, Genie, here hand-picked each and every one of y'all, and I totally trust his judgment that you are all real niggas. But I wanna get an understanding with y'all anyway. In this organization, there is no room for envy, jealousy, or individualism because you will eat and do very well for yourselves and your families. Also, there is no room for insubordination or betrayal of our trust of any kind. Whatever you're told by me, Genie, or someone else over you, it gets done, you dig? No questions asked. And lastly, there's definitely no room in this organization for fuck ups and reckless mistakes. At any point in time you put us out there in harm's way, the situation *will* get dealt with, guaranteed. Make no mistakes about it, gentlemen."

Everyone looked around and nodded their heads in agreement. "Since we all have an understanding on that, let's get down to the real reason why you're here. We have at our leisure, a product that's in very high demand and is the most sought after, best-selling commodity in the western world, mainly here in America, you dig? I'm talking Coke, gentlemen. I'm talking fish scale shit that give off a scent through metal. I'm talking the very best quality, and for you and you only, the very best price, with an abundant and consistent supply. So gentlemen, there is no reason at all why we shouldn't completely corner the market here in this city and put it on lock. And that goes for wherever else we decide to put down in the future. With the quality, availability, and the extremely good price tag on this product you'll soon be getting, you should all make out like fat cats and live well."

Everyone looked around at one another with wide smiles emerging on their faces, except for the youngster Macky Boy, who was as hard as he looked. He looked like a baby-faced assassin.

"Gentlemen, now that's the good part. Now for the not so good part. Once we put down on that type of scale and corner the entire market on every block, this will no doubt cause hatred to come our way from some cats who won't be too happy about the new reality that's about to hit the streets. So gentlemen, it goes without saying that we may have to murder some of those niggas if they get in our way, you feel me? Now it is my hope that it doesn't have to come to that, but just like with most instances when there is change, there's gonna be hatin' ass niggas standing opposing that change.

"The shit you will be getting is going to immediately disrupt business as usual in this city and beyond and for those older cats who been in power for decades. When they realize there's a new gangster on the block due to the recent demise of Mr. Ocho Rios, they will have some growing pains, you feel me?"

Tony paused as he and Genie exchanged a wicked grin. At this point every cat sitting at the table assumed that Ocho's recent demise was brought about by the very man standing before them.

"And they won't be at all receptive to that." Tony continued, "Nonetheless, it ain't nothing that we can't and won't handle when the shit come our way."

Everyone nodded in approval as Tony looked around the room at each of them, analyzing their facial expressions and body language for any objections and weaknesses.

"Are there any questions, gentlemen?" he asked. Everyone shook their heads except the Professor. "Yeah, Tony, I have a question. What about Natty Boy Ward, Cat Eye Jones, and the other Eastside cats whose toes we will be stepping on soon?" Before Tony could answer, the young brash, fearless killer out of Yonkers, Macky Boy, answered for him.

"What the fuck do you mean? Like the man just said, we will murk their asses too, if they get in our way!"

Tony gestured to the youngster to stand down. He then looked over at Genie with a smile of approval. They both liked him instantly.

"The same policy goes for them too, Professor," Tony said. "They either accept and benefit from the new reality, or like Macky Boy here just said, we murk their asses too." Everyone looked around at each in silence. "Okay gentlemen, any other questions?" No one said a word. "Alright, before we go there's one more thing. My product...I don't want it stepped on or sold over a certain price. The reason being, there is no need to. Keeping the shit as is will not only help us in our endeavor to put the city on lock and corner the market, it will also give everyone a piece of the pie so everyone can eat. I'm talking *everyone*. This will win the loyalty of the average, run of the mill street hustler. In other words, this is good public relations policy, you feel me? But again, I know there's some niggas who won't be satisfied no matter what, but that shit don't mean anything to us because this show must, and will go on. If there aren't any more questions gentlemen, this meeting is adjourned."

All of the recruits filed out of the Savoy as Tony anxiously looked down at his watch. "Well T, what kinda vibe you get from those cats?" he asked as Tony was still looking at his watch, which showed 6:25.

"Oh yeah, I get good vibes from them, Genie, especially the youngster Macky Boy."

"Yeah, I figured you would as I did when I first ran across the young nigga."

"Well do you have any recommendations regarding rank, T?" Again, Tony looked at his watch and thought to himself, *Damn! I got exactly one hour to hit a shower, get dressed then scoop Sugar up.* "Oh yeah, yeah Genie," he said when he appeared to snap back. "I think the youngster Macky Boy should be in charge of the muscle and only answer to you and me, but that's your call, bruh."

"Okay, T, what about the Professor?"

"The Professor? I think you should make him Cappo since he's a street vet and senior to the rest. But once again, Genie, you make that call since you're familiar with these niggas. Okay bruh, if there's nothing else." Tony said looking at his watch. "I gotta tear out now because that very bad broad I was telling you about earlier is waiting on a nigga to scoop her up."

"Naw. Ain't nothing else. Go do your thang, bruh." Genie smiled. With that said, Tony gave his partner dap, and tore out of the Savoy to get dressed for his date.

Chapter 11

Getting To Know You

After leaving the meeting, Tony entered his crib through the back door and conducted his ritualistic scouring of this premises. Before he could get to the bathroom, he started taking off his clothes and dropped them on the hall floor before hopping in the shower. After showering, he rushed into his huge walk-in closet that housed an extensive wardrobe, and grabbed a turquoise blue suit made by FUBU with a matching gangster lid then placed them down on his bed. Turning to his dresser, he removed a cream colored turtleneck shirt that had been folded neatly to prevent wrinkles. After sliding the turtleneck over his slender, chiseled torso, he threw on his socks, followed by his pants and matching gator boots which had the same color coordination as his suit. He then grabbed his shoulder holster which housed his two trusted twin .45s, strapped it on, threw on his suit jacket, slapped on some Gold Extreme cologne by Jay Z, followed by his jewelry. He then gave himself one last look in the mirror, and tore out for Sugar's crib.

It took Tony roughly twenty minutes to shower and get G'ed up for his date. As his canary yellow 2014 Mustang with the black racing stripes bolted onto the highway, he quickly peered at his gold, diamond studded watch. *Damn!* he thought to himself. *I have exactly fifteen minutes to get to this broad's crib and it is at least twenty minutes away.* Zooming in and out of traffic, the speedometer needle began to ease past fifty-five miles per hour. *Man I sure hope Po Po ain't out heavy this evening.* But much to his surprise, Tony was able to reach Sugar's part of town, in Crown Heights, in record time and without being given a ticket. At exactly 7:29, he was ringing Sugar's doorbell.

"Who is it?" a voiced asked on the third ring.

"It's Tony."

"Just a second," the voice said. A couple of seconds later the door slowly opened and a young female appeared, grinning. "You here for Sugar, right?" Tony smiled and nodded. "Okay. Come on in and have a seat. She's in the back getting dressed."

Tony walked in and copped a seat on a dark red leather sofa and began admiring Sugar's small, but neat, color-coordinated apartment. The apartment's theme was a mixture of authentic Ancient Egyptian and West African art. *It appears this broad is definitely up on her culture,* Tony thought to himself. *Then again, maybe she's just one of those blacks who do things not out of consciousness, but because it's the "in thing."*

Moments later, the young girl reappeared with a smile, to relay a message.

"Sugar said she will be out in a few minutes." After thanking her, Tony looked at his watch and thought to himself, *Ain't this some shit? I did all that rushing getting dressed and getting over here, risked getting a speeding ticket and the harassment that comes with that shit, and this broad ain't even finished getting dressed yet?*

However, soon after his quiet protest, Sugar emerged from the bedroom in a royal blue dress made by Dereon, looking like the owner of that clothing line. She had the look of a high powered celebrity headed to the Oscars. Seeing this, Tony rose to his feet, marveling at how the dress fit every curve and contour of her body.

With most females, their features were normally enhanced by the clothes they wear. But then there are the very few exceptions like in Sugar's case, whose beautiful, Goddess-like body, actually enhanced the look of the dress. It was very obvious to Tony and whoever had the pleasure of laying eyes on her, Sugar was no ordinary female.

"Okay, Sharonda, I'll see you later...I'm out," Sugar said to the young girl. Just before she and Tony were about to leave for their date, the young girl smiled and said in a dragging, flirtatious voice, "Byyyyeee Tooonnny."

Sugar looked back over her shoulder and smiled. "Oh yeah, Tony, this is my fast little cousin, Sharonda."

"Nice to meet you, Sharonda," Tony said before he and Sugar headed out on their date. As Tony opened Sugar's door to let her in, she carefully inspected his ride, admiring its beauty.

"Tony, this is a super nice ride you have."

"So you like it, huh?" he said, closing her door.

"Like is not the word, man. I love this car. And it's even one of my favorite colors, too."

"Thank you, babygirl. But I was certain that the royal blue you are wearing so well was your favorite color."

"Yeah, well it actually is one of my favorite colors when it comes to clothes. But as far as cars, canary yellow and red are my favorite colors."

"Well, I'm glad you like it, Sugar. Now where would you like to eat, sweetie?" he said as he backed the Mustang out of her parking lot.

"That I'm not sure, Tony. So you may wanna choose. Whatever you decide is fine with me."

"Okay, I know just the place, I think you will like it." He smiled at her. "Have you ever eaten Japanese food before, Sugar?"

"Sure. Sounds good to me," she said with a slight degree of apprehension on her face. After a few minutes of driving, Tony's Mustang pulled into the parking lot of Amura, a traditional and sophisticated Japanese restaurant on the upper east side of Manhattan. Once inside, he and Sugar were met by a young Japanese hostess dressed in traditional Japanese garb.

CATO

"Hello, how are you this even-ing? Dinner for two?" She spoke with a thick Japanese accent.

"Yes," Tony replied.

"Would you and your wife like Sushi bar or Hibachi grill, sir?"

"We'll have Hibachi, please."

"Follow me, please, sir." The petite Japanese girl said as she led them into a huge dining room occupied exclusively by white people. Almost immediately, Tony and Sugar were met with long, intense stares. After being seated, Sugar smiled and glanced at Tony with a slight uneasiness on her face.

"Do you get the feeling we're being watched?" she asked under her breath. They both chuckled.

"Maybe they're just intrigued by us. But then again, they may even think we're celebrities or something."

"Maybe so, but I really think it has more to do with the fact we're the only spots in here."

Tony casually looked around the room and facetiously said, "Naaaw. You think so?" Once again they chuckled. Moments later, a short and stocky Japanese waiter walked up to the table asking, "What can I get you to drink this eve-ning?" He gave them a pleasant smile.

"I'll have hot tea," Tony answered. The waiter then turned to Sugar.

"And for you, ma'am?"

"I'll have a Hennessy and Coke on the rocks, please."

"Okay, thank-a-you. I shall return with your bev-e-rages in one moment," he said before walking away. Sugar slowly scanned the dining room and noticed that the many stares by the white diners persisted.

"Tony. How often do you come here?" she asked.

"Only on special occasions like tonight." He smiled. "If you are alluding to the looks we are getting, being a black man who frequent places most blacks do not, I'm used to it."

"Mmmm hmmmm." she said giving a fake smile to the staring white folks. "Do you normally get these kind of looks when you do come here?"

"Yeah, but that's pretty much anywhere I go that most black folks don't normally frequent. Japanese cuisine is not exactly a staple of black folks diets, you know?"

You ain't lying, Sugar thought to herself. Moments later, the waiter returned with their drinks and took their appetizer and dinner order. Tony ordered a Black Dragon roll for himself and shrimp tempura for Sugar who made strong objections against eating anything raw and much to Tony's amusement. Once the appetizers made it to their table, the sight of sushi caused an extensive line of wrinkles to form on Sugar's face as if she bit down on a lemon.

"What is that?" she asked.

"It's called a Black Dragon roll."

"Is any of it uncooked?" she asked with her face still wrinkled up.

"No." He laughed and said, "It's shrimp fried in a special batter encased in rice with barbecued eel on top. And it's *like that* believe it or not. Would you care to try some?"

"Nah, I'll pass," she said with her hands waving in front of her wrinkled up face.

"Are you going to try your shrimp tempura? You did say you liked shrimp, right?"

"Yeah I love shrimp, but what is shrimp tem...tem...tem...who?" Tony laughed and then sounded out the word for her.

"Tem-pur-a. Tempura. It's just shrimp fried in a special batter like the Dragon roll, but it's cool. Try it. I think you will like it."

Sugar looked at him with a degree of apprehension and picked up a piece of the tempura.

"Okay. What do I do with it now?" she asked, clutching the roll.

"Now, you just take it and dip it into this sauce here." She followed his instructions and dunked the tempura into the sauce then slowly thrust it towards her slightly opened mouth with her eyes fixed on Tony. When she bit down on the battered shrimp, the look of approval began to replace the remaining wrinkles on her face as her eyes began to sparkle. Tony braced for her reaction.

"Well? You like it?" he asked. She nodded her head and kept on chewing.

"Ummm. This is not bad at all. In fact, this is very good," she said, picking up another piece then repeating the same technique.

"Okay, that's what's up. Now since you're being a little adventurous tonight, why don't you try a California roll."

"A California what?" she asked in an animated voice with the wrinkles beginning to reappear in her forehead. Sugar's slight outburst caused the return of another round of stares and gazes from the intrigued white diners. Tony smiled and peered around the restaurant.

"It's called a California roll," he whispered. "It's just crab and avocado wrapped in rice. And rest your nerves. It's not raw." He chuckled.

"Okay now, are you sure it's not that raw shit?"

"I'm positive it's not the raw shit." He laughed. "It's very much cooked. I wouldn't lie to you." Tony was extremely amused at this extremely beautiful, yet unrefined black woman sitting next to him who kept it real and didn't pretend to be something that she wasn't.

"Well....okay. I guess I can try it since you said it's cooked," she said cautiously.

"It's cooked, baby, I can assure you," he said, laughing as he motioned to the waiter and ordered the roll. Moments later, the waiter returned with the roll.

"I hope you enjoy," he said before walking away. Once again, Sugar thoroughly examined the rolls as her eyes rotated between them and Tony.

"Okay, Tony, now what is that green stuff?"

"The green stuff, as you so cutely referred to it, is called Wasabi. It's made from a plant of the Brassicaceae family, which includes cabbages, horseradish, and mustard. It has an aromatic taste to it. In other words, it will open up your sinuses, so be careful. The pink stuff is called pickled ginger root. They both compliment the taste of the sushi. And this is how you eat it. You take the Wasabi, or the green stuff as you called it…" Sugar snickered "…and you mix it with this soy sauce here. Then you take the roll and dip it into the mixture just like you did with the tempura, and you place it into your mouth." Reaching over, Tony gently placed the roll between Sugar's slightly parted, voluptuous lips. With her eyes glued on Tony, she cautiously bit down and began chewing, and almost immediately, he could see that it was pleasing to her taste buds just like the tempura.

"Okay. Okay. It's pretty good as well," she said, nodding her head. "Not bad. Not bad at all. But...but...something the green shit is opening up my sinuses sumpin' serious!" she said looking as though she was about to sneeze. Tony laughed.

"I told you, baby. That wasabi ain't no joke. Remember I told you it's very aromatic. Okay now, here's where the pink stuff comes in," he said as he placed a piece of the ginger root in her mouth to counteract the pungent taste of the wasabi.

"Ummm! Okay," she said smiling. "The pink stuff, or the pickled ginger root, serves its purpose. Okay. I like the California roll, but I really dig the shrimp tem...tem..."

Tony assisted her again in sounding it out. "Tem-pur-a. Say it with me." Sounding the word out they both said at the same time. "Tem-pur-a. Okay. Now again, Tem-pur-a. Tempura. Now you say it by yourself this time." Tony said.

"Tem-pur-a. Tempura!"

"There you go, Miss Jones. I think you got it now. For a project girl from Florida, you did good." He chuckled.

After finishing off the last sushi roll, the Hibachi chef rolled out with his food cart of various ingredients and put on a dazzling display of juggling, fancy dicing, and culinary pyrotechnics. Having never witnessed anything like this before, and let alone eating at a Japanese restaurant, Sugar was extremely impressed with the demonstration. Sensing her lack of knowledge about Japanese cuisine, Tony explained to her the years of extensive training a Hibachi chef must go through in order to reach that level.

After finishing off the main course, and after a couple of more rounds of Hen and Coke for Sugar, she began to feel the effects of it, which caused her to loosen up a little as the stares from the white folks commenced. Noticing the stares, she looked around the dining room and said under her breath, "Tony, you got me in here in this sophisticated restaurant, occupied by all these uppity ass crackers, acting ghetto." Tony laughed.

"Well you did say you were 'project raised,' right?"

Popping her neck she said, "Yep! Show you right! Which means I don't mind cutting either." They both then burst out laughing so loud that the waiter and restaurant manager peeped their heads around the corner and said something to each Japanese. A white lady sitting at the table over from them with her husband, who had been one of the main ones staring at them since they walked in the door, finally built up the nerve to say something.

"Ma'am, excuse me. May I ask you a personal question if you don't mind?"

Before answering Sugar mumbled under her breath to Tony. "Ohhh shit! Let me break out the straight razor!" Tony smiled and gave her a slight nudge under the table.

"No, ma'am, I don't mind," Sugar said with a fake, toothy smile on her face.

"Where did you get that dress? It is sooo beautiful, and you look absolutely stunning in it!"

"Oh yes, my dear. I purchased it during my recent trip to Dubai this past summer," Sugar said in a bouergie voice.

"You've been to Dubai?" the white lady asked in surprise. She was completely turned around in her chair at this point.

"Oh yes, dear. My husband and I have been there thrice. In fact, we make it our business to travel abroad every summer." This seemed to excite the white woman to the point she began jumping up and down in her chair clasping her hands together as if she was in church.

"My husband and I are planning our own trip abroad to Paris this spring. It will be our first trip and I am so, so excited!"

"Oh that's just fabulous, darling." Sugar said. "We've been to Paris more times that I can count on two hands. And shopped at nearly every boutique in Paris' city limits."

"Wow!" the excited white woman said as she moved about in her chair. Tony sipped his tea and stared straight ahead trying his damnedest to contain his laughter. He was on the verge of literally falling out of his seat. Sugar was feeding some serious bullshit to the nosey white woman and she woofed every bit of it down as she became more and more excited with every serving. "So what do you and your husband do?" she asked Sugar. Tony sipped on his tea again and cut his eyes back at Sugar bracing for her response.

Without missing a beat and with the fake smile still intact, Sugar rattled off, "My husband is a record executive for Roca-Fella Records, owned by Jay Z, and is their chief accountant."

Tony thought to himself, *Damn this bitch is a trip!* At this point the nosey white woman's husband who was fed up with his wife's prying, or perhaps with Sugar's bullshit, decided to intervene.

"Honey! Would you please let those nice people finish their meals. Hello, how are you?" he said as he stood up and extended his hand out to Tony. "I'm Aaron Goldman and this is my very inquisitive wife, Helen."

"I'm Antonio Stallworth." Tony said, shaking his hand. "And this here is...

"And I'm his wife, Constance Stallworth. Nice to meet you," Sugar said. Tony was about to die inside from laughter. Goldman then reached into his wallet and handed Tony a business card before returning to his seat. "I'm a local criminal attorney for both federal and state offenses. But God forbid if you ever need my services."

"Thank you," Tony said after quickly scanning the card before sliding it into his pocket."

"Mr. and Mrs. Stallworth, can you please forgive my wife? She can get a little carried away sometimes, especially when the subject of shopping abroad comes up."

"Oh I don't mind, Mr. Goldman. I really enjoyed my little discourse with Helen regarding my many past excursions abroad in times gone by."

Moving quickly to put an end to Sugar's performance before he laughed in those white folks faces, Tony motioned for the waiter. "I'm ready to cash out now," he said. After taking care of the tab and leaving the tip, Tony and Sugar stood up from the table.

Gangsta Shyt

"It was nice meeting you, Mr. and Mrs. Goldman," Tony said as he shook Goldman's hand again.
"Likewise, Mr. Stallworth." Just before exiting the Hibachi room, Sugar capped her impromptu performance by peering back at the white woman and saying aloud, wiggling her fingers, "*Titulo, Helen!*"
She and Tony then strolled away arm-in-arm like a celebrity couple, while all eyes were trained on them. Once outside, Tony nearly collapsed to the pavement as he doubled over in laughter.
"Girl! You are a straight fucking fool!" He said as he attempted to catch his breath. As they both laughed loudly and fell into each other, passersby stared at them as they were going to and from the restaurant.
"Well, Mr. Stallworth, how would you rate my performance? Do I deserve an Oscar or what?"
After finally catching his breath, and regaining his composure, he answered, "You definitely get my vote, Mrs. Constance Stallworth." They both laughed aloud again.
Clutching Sugar's arm, he said, "Girl, come on here. Ole crazy ass woman. Let's tear before these folks call security on us for disturbing the peace." Arm-in-arm they made their way to Tony's ride, climbed into it, and sped away from the scene still laughing at tonight's events.
As the song *I Can't Feel My Face* by the Weeknd played on the radio, Tony asked, "Sugar, are you ready to go home now?"
"Nah, not really, Tony. It's still kinda early for me. Why? Are you ready for me to go home or sumpin'?" she asked jokingly.
"No, of course not," he said laughing. "You're entertaining me. In fact, this is the most I've laughed in quite a while."
"Well, maybe it's because you're too serious and uptight all the time." She smiled.
"That's a fair assessment. But maybe all I needed was someone like you to take me outta that mindset."

"Okay, Mr. Smooth talker, I hear you," she said smiling. "Now what did you have in my mind? Oh wait, think I need to clarify that, I mean what would you like to do tonight?" Tony laughed.

"Okay. Would you like to go someone and listen to some music?"

"Sure sir, that's cool."

"Okay, Ms. Jones, I have just the place. Have you ever been to or heard of the Calypso?"

"Yeah, I've heard of it before and was supposed to go a little while back, but Wanda had car trouble so we didn't make it out. I heard it is a real nice spot."

"You heard right. It is the biggest and nicest club in the city. Do you like to listen to old school music?"

"Sure. Who don't? My uncle used to play it all the time when I was a shorty back in Orlando."

"Okay. Cool," Tony said as he maneuvered his ride in and out of the lanes.

Within a few minutes, Tony pulled into the Calypso's parking lot. After he and Sugar stepped out of the Mustang, they could clearly hear every sad lyric in the song, *By The Time I Get To Arizona* by Isaac Hayes, coming from inside the club. Once they made it inside, they found a pretty nice crowd. There were people on the dance floor getting their collective groove on, while some sat at tables and others in the large game room playing pool.

"Wow, Tony!" Sugar said, as she scanned the huge club. This place is super nice!"

"Yeah, we did some major renovations to it a little while back."

"We? So you own this place, Tony?" she asked.

"Yeah. I'm actually a silent partner with the DJ's brother. Let's go grab a table, Sugar," he said. As they headed to the back of the club to grab a table, the DJ, Tracy T, gave Tony a shout out.

"What's goin' down, Mr. Antonio Stallworth! How ya livin'?"

Tony responded by throwing up the clinched fist before he and Sugar sat down. A young waitress sporting a tall, but neatly formed, afro walked up. "Can I get you two something to drink?" she asked.

"Yes," Sugar said, "I'll have a Hennessey and Coke on the rocks, please."

"And what can I get for you, Mr. Stallworth?"

"Now you know I don't drink, so I will take the usual."

"Oh yeah." She giggled. "I forgot. Club soda with cherries. Be back in a minute," she said before walking off to the next table.

"Tony, do they always play old school music here?" Sugar asked, popping her fingers and moving her head to the music.

"Pretty much. We cater more so to the old school crowd here at this one. You know we have another one over in the Bed Stuy that caters to the younger hip hop crowd."

"No, I didn't know that. This is *nice*. I would rather come here than where the younger crowd hangs out at. My granny once told me I was an old soul because of the way I conducted myself and my preference for old things such as cars, movies and music."

"Is that right? I was told the same thing by my uncle. Now don't get me wrong, I am from the hip hop, gangsta rap era, but I do like to mellow out with some old school sometimes," he said as the song, *Don't Stop To You Get Enough* by Michael Jackson played. After the waitress returned with their drinks, the sizing up process began.

"Ms. Jones, tell me a little about yourself," Tony asked.

"What do you wanna know?" she smiled and asked.

"Everything that there is to know. I want to hear all about it," he said, smiling and looking into her eyes intently.

"Okay, let me see...I'm originally from Orlando, Florida born and raised. My grandparents raised me and my brother after my parents died in a car wreck when I was eight. My grandmother is still in Orlando, and my grandfather died shortly after I graduated from high school. Sometime later, I moved here with my Aunt Helen, Sharonda's mother, to attend college at Columbia University on academic and athletic scholarships."

"An athletic scholarship?" Tony asked in surprise.

"Yes, that's right, Mr. Stallworth. Remember I told you the other night that I was a high school track star. I was also a basketball star."

"Yeah, I recall you telling me about you being a track star." Tony said smiling. "But I didn't know you were are a three sport athlete in high school."

"Yep! That's right, sir. Okay. Now where was I?" Sugar said after taking a sip of Hen and Coke.

"You moved here to attend college," Tony reminded her.

"Oh yeah. Well that was the plan initially, but I became involved with someone who turned out to be a big distraction and I got sidetracked for a couple years and dropped out of school. But, after finally coming to my senses and dropping him, I re-enrolled to complete my accounting degree and now I'm very close to finishing. Okaaaaay. Let's see what else," she said. "I'm twenty-six. I'm single, and I don't have any kids. So I guess that sums up my life story. Pretty boring, huh?" Tony sipped his club soda with his eyes fixed on her without blinking.

"Okay now that we got that out of the way, Mr. Stallworth. You just heard my story, now let's have yours," she smiled and said. The attraction they had for each other seemed to build with each question and comment.

"Well, I'm originally from Detroit, Michigan, but I moved here with my parents when I was twelve. My father was murdered two years later and my mother who had never known another man, died less than one year later of a broken heart. After being orphaned, my father's brother, Uncle Walt, who taught me a lot, became like a father to me. Uncle Walt made sure I had everything I needed, kept me in line, and kept me in school even though he was a busy man who was deeply involved in his lifestyle. Now this was during the time I was fastly becoming a juvenile delinquent, due to the strong allure of gangs and all the other shit that a young black male is exposed to in a huge city like New York. Soooo, after miraculously graduating from high school, I joined the Marine Corp, then fresh outta boot camp I was shipped to a small little hellish place called, Afghanistan. While I was away, my uncle and mentor, Walt, was murdered," Tony said as he momentarily paused in deep reflection. He sipped on his soda as Sugar's eyes were fixated on him.

Detecting his pain, Sugar asked, "Were your uncle and father's murderers ever found?" Tony's green eyes narrowed into tiny slits as he seemed to be reliving the two tragedies.

"Ummm well.....yeah." His voice was distant. "Yeah they were found alright," he said, chillingly, as he sipped his soda with a thousand mile stare in his eyes, reflecting back to that night they were found and who found them. Unbeknownst to Sugar, the very man sitting in front of her was the one who found the men responsible for murdering two of the three people he loved more than anyone or anything else in this world. And that's what made it gratifying when he in turn took their lives, along with some of their muscle.

The events that led to his father and uncle's murders were set into motion when his father, Lett Stallworth, was contracted by some syndicate cats to put in some work back in Detroit. True to his rep, Lett took care of his business, but was never paid the balance of his bread. After a few unsuccessful attempts to collect, the cats who owed him became a little agitated and thus concluded that it would be more feasible to just hire some other hitter to cancel out Lett for a mere fraction of what was owed to him. But as the old saying goes, you get what you pay for.

It turned out that the young ambitious killer contracted to waste Lett was nothing more than a rank amateur who had his new career cut short before it got off the ground, thanks to Lett, the professional. After the failed attempt on his life, Lett took his grievance to another level by paying his debtors a visit late one evening at their hangout. Before the evening was over, Lett collected his bread, in addition to severance and retirement pay, while five people lost their lives in the process. Two big timers and three of their soldiers. Immediately thereafter, it was time for Lett and his family to flip the script. So he packed up his wife and only son and relocated to Brooklyn where his older brother, another gangster, resided. Within two years of the move, and beginning of a new life with his family made possible by the quarter mil he guerillaed from the syndicate cats, Lett Stallworth paid for it with his life. And a few years later, so did his brother Walt.

Starting with the revenge killings of his loved ones murders began Antonio Stallworth's career as a killer for scriller. So like father, like uncle, like son, being a killer for scriller seemed to be encoded in the Stallworth DNA. As the song *It's A Man's World* by the Godfather of Soul, James Brown, blared from the club's speakers, Tony's mind seemed to be marooned on a faraway planet, in another place and time. He seemed to totally forget that Sugar was still sitting in front of him. Realizing that her inquiries into the deaths of his father and uncle had touched a deep and sensitive nerve, Sugar acted quickly to change the mood.

"Hey, Mr. Stallworth!" she said smiling. "Can a chick like me get a dance, sir?" Almost instantly, Tony's stone-cold expression transformed into a smile, as if nothing ever happened.

"Sure, babygirl. It would be my honor and pleasure to dance with a fine and beautiful chick like you." With that said, they made their way to the semi-crowded dance floor arm and arm as they were met with stares and gazes. It seemed like every cat in the Calypso was gawking at Sugar with lust, and every broad hissed with jealousy at Sugar. It was obvious to everyone, broads and dudes alike, Sugar was indeed the baddest, finest bitch in the entire spot. As they took to the dance floor and began dancing in front of a captivated audience, Tony and Sugar danced to *Keep On Truckin'* by Eddie Kendricks formerly of the Temptations. After one more dance, they returned to their table.

"So you're going to be an accountant, huh?" Tony asked.

"Yes sir," she answered proudly.

"That's what's up, Sugar," he said. "But you know, that's very surprising to me."

"Why is that? Because I'm from the projects?" she asked, popping her neck. Tony laughed aloud with his hands up in front of him.

"No! No! I didn't mean it like that, babygirl. What I meant was, a beautiful black woman like yourself could very easily become a big time model and grace the cover of Jet or Ebony, but instead you opted to become an accountant."

"Oh okay. I thought I was about to do some cuttin.' Way to clean that up though."

"Oh no, Miss Jones," he said laughing. "I'm ain't trying to get cut."

"But seriously, Tony, I'm very close to taking my final exams in a couple months."

"And I am impressed, Miss Jones. Wow! I'm actually chilling with and sitting next to a future certified accountant. And a very beautiful one at that."

"Okay, Mr. Smooth talker. I'm sure you tell all the females that shit."

"Yeah, but never one that was an accountant," he said before they both laughed again as Sugar landed a playful punch to his arm.

"But for real for real, Sugar, that's a very big accomplishment and you should be very proud of yourself."

"Now wait a minute, Tony. I'm not an accountant just yet. I still have to pass those exams, you know." She looked up as the waitress placed her Hennessy and Coke down in front of her.

"Well, you got this. I have confidence that you'll ace those exams, because I know a sharp and intelligent black woman when I see one."

"Thanks, Tony. I hope you're right, because I've been having some serious butterflies just thinking about those exams." Tony could clearly see the anxiety in her eyes

"Sugar, that's a natural reaction, so don't worry. There's an old saying once told to me by a very wise man and mentor: "What you put into a thing, that's what you will get out of it." In other words, since you put in a lot of time and hard work into reaching your goals of being an accountant, when the time comes it will pay off."

"Thank you, Tony, for having confidence in me," she said smiling. "I really needed that." Sugar wasn't used to encouragement from guys regarding her education. Typically, what she found with most brothers, they were intimidated by that.

"And you are so very welcome, babygirl," he said smiling.

A short time later, after the club had started to get packed, Tony and Sugar tore out and headed to Sugar's crib. Within a few minutes, they pulled up in front of her apartment.

"I really, really enjoyed my evening with you, Miss Jones," Tony said.

"Likewise, Mr. Stallworth. I really had a nice time with you as well." He leaned over and placed a gentle kiss on her cheek.

"When will I be able to lay eyes on you again, Miss Jones?" he asked in his player's voice.

"Whenever you have time out from your busy schedule, Mr. Stallworth," she said smiling.

"For someone as fine, intelligent, funny, and beautiful as you, I will definitely make time."

"Okay, Mr. Stallworth, we'll see. You have my number." After escorting her to her front door, they embraced and parted ways.

On the way back to his crib, Tony wore a smile the whole way there as he listened to the old school joint *Me and My Girlfriend by 2 Pac* on the satellite radio. By two chance encounters, and for the first time in his life, Tony had met a woman that genuinely stimulated and aroused his curiosity, more so than Angela. Constance Jones, or Sugar as she called herself, was certainly no ordinary woman. She was beautiful. Fine. Intelligent. Feisty. Gutsy. Hip, and exuded a charisma and confidence of a woman who knew exactly what she wanted in life and where she was going. These were the qualities in a woman that men like Tony so greatly desired and were in constant pursuit of. Now for Tony, that pursuit may have just ended. After reaching his crib and entering through the back door as usual, then performing the ritualistic scouring of each room, Tony undressed, slid his two .45s under his pillow then melted into his bed. Before drifting off to sleep, one last pleasant thought for the evening entered his mind that brought a wide smile to his face. The one woman who possessed all those desirable qualities, would soon be his.

CATO

Chapter 12
Straight From the Jungles of Bogota

Early the next morning, Tony was awakened by Tupac's Gangster Party ringtone.

"What's up?" he answered in a groggy voice.

"Hello, my friend! How are you this morning?"

"Oh I'm good, Mando." He rolled over and peered at the clock to see it was exactly 5:48 a.m.

"Well, my friend, before Armando tells you what is going on, I want you to know what you did the other night was a thing of beauty! In fact my friend, it made the news even here."

Tony cracked a sinister grin. "Why thank you, Mando. I'm glad you enjoyed it."

"Now, my friend, for the main reason Armando awakened you so early this morning. Would you look out of your window at your driveway." Tony followed his instructions and looked out of his front window to see a huge moving truck parked in his driveway with a driver sitting in the front seat. It totally caught him off guard.

"Is that the…….."

"Si Si, my friend. That is the load," Armando interjected.

"Damn, Mando!" Tony said in amazement. "You don't be bullshittin' around do you?" Armando laughed.

"No! No, my friend! Armando never bullshits when it comes to business."

"Damn!" Tony said to himself.

"Also, my friend, you will find I included a small bonus for that thing of beauty. The driver has been instructed to transport the cargo to the place of your choosing. So be safe, and Armando will hear from you soon enough, my friend."

"Okay Mando, later." Tony stood there with the cell phone still in his hand, and still looking at the huge moving truck in disbelief. After getting over the initial shock, he placed a call to Genie. On about the eighth ring Genie finally picked up.

"Yeah! Who the fuck is this?" Genie said.

"Hey, nigga, wake your ass up!" Tony said, laughing. "It's game on, nigga." Genie wiped his eyes so he could focus on the clock.

"Huh? What's game on?" he asked.

"You know, bruh. That thing from the jungle we been waiting on."

"Ohhhhhh okay. You mean, it's here?"

"Already, nigga!"

"Oh okay, T. Well, what do you need me to do, T?"

"I need you to get your ass over here ASAP, nigga." Tony smiled and said. "I'm getting nervous as fuck having this shit sitting here in my driveway." Still in disbelief, Genie peered over at the clock again tripping on how early it was.

"Hey! Genie Boy! Are you still there, bruh? Wake up, negro!"

"Yeah! Yeah, T! I'm still here man. A nigga just still trying to wake-up. Thought I was dreaming or some shit."

"No bruh, you ain't dreaming, I can promise you that. This is the real deal, my nigga. Now go throw some water on your face and get over here."

"Okay, T. I'll be at you in a minute." After hanging up the phone, Tony walked over to the stereo and hit the play button. The song *Let's Get It* by Young Jeezy bumped from the speakers. As Tony stood there soaking in the song's relevant lyrics and thinking about the new era in which he was to embark on, he couldn't help but smile. Just as Armando Chavez had promised, the load arrived in exactly one week, but much to Tony's pleasant surprise it had arrived right on his fucking front doorstep as big as day in broad day light.

Within twenty minutes, Genie walked through Tony's front door looking behind him.

"Hey, T, is that the shit outside, man?" Tony smiled and nodded his head without saying a word.

"*Damn!*" Genie said. "Your man don't be bullshittin,' do he?"

"Nope. Not at all." He gave a brief smile then quickly switched to business mode. "Okay, bruh, we need to go ahead and stash that shit away. It's making me super nervous just sitting there."

"Okay, T, let's do this shit."

"I'll have the driver to follow us there," Tony said as he set his house alarm before walking out of the door. After instructing the driver, Tony and Genie pulled out of the driveway and headed to the stash spot with the precious cargo behind them.

Half an hour later, Tony, Genie and the cargo arrived at Genie's aunt and uncle's property. After his aunt passed away and his uncle was put in a nursing home due to Alzheimer's, he'd inherited the property. The property had a huge brick home that looked as if it was still being occupied due to Genie keeping it up. It also had a huge utility shed, a climate controlled barn that sat about seventy-five yards from the house, and four huge, highly trained German Shepherds that looked like wolves, who were on constant patrol of the property. After unloading the cargo into the barn, and concealing it inside bales of hay, the driver drove away, leaving Genie looking at Tony standing there in utter disbelief.

"T, I counted at least fifteen hundred keys, man."

"Yeah, my man included a bonus for, as he termed it, 'that thing of beauty' last week." They both chuckled.

"T, man, it looks like we got our work cut out for us." Genie shook his head.

"Yeah, bruh, I believe you're right. But at least we will get paid."

In more ways than one, we will have our work cut out for us, Tony thought to himself. He knew what typically came with this new line of work - hatred and animosity. But he was up for the task. He was resolute in dealing with whatever challenges came his way, including any and all drama.

Chapter 13

The New Reality Hit the Streets

Once Tony's organization introduced his low-priced, high-quality, uncut, unadulterated product to the streets, the impact was felt almost immediately. On every block in the hood, his product was being peddled by every hustler from the kilo dealer, to the quarter key cats, to the ounce dealer, all the way down to the gram pushers. This takeover was utter and complete.

The void left by Ocho's departure had now been filled. The *new reality* as Tony termed it, reverberated beyond the city and into New Jersey, Connecticut, and even into Virginia, Philly, and Baltimore. As a result, the small pockets of competition began to quickly evaporate, making Tony the undisputed cocaine distributor in the city and perhaps in the tri-states and beyond. But just as Tony had predicted, his *new reality* had begun to cause resentment and animosity, particularly amongst some of the O.G.s.

Nathan "Natty Boy" Ward, the founder and leader of a powerful black syndicate, for years had all five boroughs on lock during their Ocho's reign. But now that shit was over with Tony's arrival. Now in the undignified position of no longer being on the top of the cash pile, and relegated to subordinate role of purchasers, this did not sit too well with the O.Gs and would perhaps soon be the catalyst for some gangster shit. As Tony tightened up his grip on the streets, he also continued to tighten his grip on his relationship with Sugar, just as he was about to bring another relationship to a sad close.

CATO

Chapter 14

Walk Away From Love

On June 2nd, the day of Angela's birthday, which was also the day before she was set to leave the country for her new job in Germany, Tony treated her to dinner at another one of her favorite Italian restaurants, Sweet Basil's. Tony hired an Italian band to serenade her, and had a florist to deliver her two and a half dozen blood red roses, which represented her age of thirty. To culminate the special birthday dinner, Tony handed her a gold five carat diamond watch with a matching necklace which caused her to become emotional.

"This is the most memorable birthday I've ever had Tony," she said with her voice cracking. "Thank you Tony." She kissed him on the cheek.

"You are more than welcome, baby. I thought you'd like it."

"Yes, Tony! Like? *I love it!* It's beautiful. And the dinner, the roses, the serenade, I love it all. But more than anything, I love you, baby." She kissed him again.

After dinner, Tony took Angela to her favorite place on Orchard beach, and for several minutes they walked in the beach sand holding hands in complete silence. In the backdrop, the full moon illuminated the night and the stars dotted the heavens like tiny lanterns. The few couples who were there sat on blankets in full romantic mode. After walking in silence through the course beach sands, whose texture was like grains of salt, in what may have very well been their last romantic outing, Angela broke the silence.

· "Tony, I'm ready to go now." She stared into his eyes, speaking in a serious voice, "I want you to take me home and make love to me like you've never done before."

Facing her, Tony smiled and tilted his gangster lid. "Your wish is my command, Miss Washington."

A short time later, Tony took her to her crib and gave her what she wanted, while the song *Like I'm Gonna Lose You* by Meghan Trainor featuring John Legend, played in the background. For the rest of the night, Tony made love to Angela properly, just as she requested.

Early the next morning, Tony helped Angela pack the last of her belongings as a team of professional movers began to empty out her house. It was a very sad occasion for both Tony and Angela because they understood that their lives were now at a crossroad. Tony knew in his mind that their five year, on again off again relationship had run its course and this move for Angela was the proverbial end of story for their romance. Tony also knew in his heart that he had finally found that special woman that for the first time in his life genuinely sparked his interest. And that special woman's name was Sugar.

After the last piece of furniture was loaded onto the eighteen wheeler, rendering Angela's crib an empty hull, she and Tony climbed into his ride and began the sad journey to the airport.

En route to the airport, the old school satellite radio station played *Walk Away From Love* by David Ruffin. As Mr. Ruffin sang the heartbreak and sadness of walking away from a love affair, his lyrics seemed to penetrate deep into Angela's heart as her eyes began to well up with tears. Seeing this, Tony gently held her hand as he drove, but he elected not to say anything. He knew that this was one of those moments where things were better left unsaid, because no words in the English language would make shit better or soften the blow to Angela's heart. So the only thing he did at that point was just hold her hand as she sobbed openly with her head against his shoulder.

Once they finally made it to the airport, Tony grabbed her luggage and took it to the baggage check in. Afterwards, he and

Angela aimlessly walked through the airport holding hands without saying much of anything until it was time for her to board the plane that would soon carry her to a new life and a new beginning. Following a few more minutes of spending their last moments together in quiet reflection, and holding hands tightly, the voice over the loudspeaker said, "Now boarding flight 737 to Hamburgh, Germany!"

After a long, sensual, passionate kiss, Tony and Angela said their goodbyes, and parted ways out of each others' lives. Angela to a new country and a new chapter, and Tony to a new era and chapter as well, but perhaps with a new woman.

Later that evening, Tony sat alone at the Calypso listening to the sorrowful wail of Al Green's song, *For the Good Times*, blare from the jukebox as he waited for his partner, Genie, to arrive and brief him on the matters of his illicit trade. The ramifications of his *new reality* was beginning to come full circle as the ugly head of jealousy, envy, and discontent amongst the O.G. syndicate cats had begun to show itself, just as Tony had predicted. Therefore, he knew he needed to act fast to prevent the inevitable shedding of blood which was a life he had left behind and had no intentions of ever revisiting. Now more than ever, he had an extra incentive and motivation to never look back.

"What's up, T?" Genie said as he walked into the Calypso.

"Just chillin,' Genie. Just chillin,' bruh. How's everything on the street?"

"Other than a little beef coming from those O.G. syndicate niggas, everythang is Gucci. But them niggas will be alright though." Genie quipped before pouring himself a drink. Hearing this, Tony shook his head with obvious disgust.

"You know, Genie, I knew this shit would happen with those O.Gs, and I told you this shit from the beginning. But I was hoping that I was wrong this time."

"Well, *fuck'em!*" Genie said before turning up his drink. "Those poo butt as niggas have it better now than they ever did! I think they have outlived their day anyway. So why in the fuck are they still catching beef?" Tony looked at him and began to explain in a contemptuous tone.

"You see, Genie, my brother, it's like this. Niggas don't like to see their own kind be successful and this shit goes all the way back to slavery, and believe it or not, that slavery shit still affects our people to this very day. Today you have black people and you have niggas. The black people like you and me, want to have something and want to see other blacks have something. But niggas on the other hand, don't want to see me, you, and even other niggas have shit. This type of slave mentality has plagued our people for over four hundred years and to keep it real, still plagues us today. And what compounds this problem is the same as it was back during slavery. You have older niggas hating on younger niggas. As long as Ocho Rios, who was not black, was their plug everyone, including those syndicate niggas, was happy and content with that shit. But now that one of their own, a black man, a young black man, is the new gangster on the block, they're unhappy and discontented, even though like you stated earlier, they have it much better now than they did under Ocho, who was pimping them."

"I know, T. Ain't that a bitch, mayne!" Genie said after quickly downing another drink.

"Yeah it is, Genie, and I see where this shit is headed. So what I want you to do is to contact Mr. Ward and arrange a meeting with him and his associates here at 7 p.m. sharp tomorrow. Time to have a heart to heart talk with these old niggas."

"Okay, T. What good will it do? I'm not at all optimistic, bruh." After Genie exited the Calypso, Tony sat pondering the weight of Genie's words. *What good will it do?* But that was classic Genie Boy, the pessimist. Of the two, Tony was always the optimistic one, even though he was the cold blooded killer. However, on this rare occasion he shared Genie's pessimism, because something in his gut instincts told him that he was just wasting his time trying to placate those ungrateful niggas, and would just end up murdering them anyway. But then again, that could just be the instinctual dark side of a killer for scriller. *Handle your business, and send marks to the meet their makers. Nothing personal, and nothing to do with emotions, just business.* But that was the side Tony was doing his damnedest to put behind him, but fuck niggas was making that hard.

CATO

Chapter 15

It's Official! Sugar is Tony's Woman Now

Later that evening, around a quarter to eight, Tony scooped Sugar up from her crib and took her to dinner and a movie. Though Tony was thrown for a loop with the departure of Angela out of his life, he didn't waste any time filling the void. Besides, he just wasn't the grieving type. He lived by a creed that life must and will go on. After the movies, he and Sugar headed to a penthouse party hosted by a local young white politician who was fascinated with Tony, not to mention in his hip pocket. As soon as Tony and Sugar stepped into the joint, all eyes were trained on them due to Tony's celebrity-like status. Every room they walked into, there were people openly snorting lines of his coke and smoking weed, including some of those local politicians.

"Heeeeeey Tony!" the young congressman, Josh Daniels said. "Come over here. I have some folks I want you to meet." Tony and Sugar joined him. "This here is Tony Stallworth." Daniels said to this tall white man who smelled like a cop.

"Tony, this is District Attorney Courtland Franks."

"Nice to meet you, Mr. Stallworth," the prosecutor said, shaking his hand. Tony nodded and gave Daniels that look like *what the fuck?* Daniels laughed and pulled him to the side.

"Dude, don't trip," he said laughing. "He's on our team, baby. You know I wouldn't put you out there. By the way, he's got a 200 dollar a day coke habit. *Your* coke," he said in drunken laughter.

"Alright, Josh. I done told you, you better chill with this gangster fantasy of yours in public. You gone fuck around and get caught up," Tony said, smiling and patting him on his back.

"Bro, I got this. I have congressional immunity. You ain't know?" he said in a black man's accent.

"Okay, Josh. I hear ya, kid." Tony looked at Sugar, shaking his head. "Hey Josh, I will holla at you later, kid. Me and my old lady about to tear out."

"Well damn, Tony. Where are your manners? You didn't introduce us. She's freaking beautiful!" he said as he tried to kiss Sugar on her cheek. Tony got in between him.

"Alright, Josh, don't make me pistol whip you, kid," Tony said smiling. "We will talk later. If you need something, holla at my folks.

"Okay, bet that up, bro," Josh said. "But you ain't gotta pistol whip me over your wife. You know I don't roll like that," he yelled as Tony and Sugar walked away.

Once they reached Tony's car, Sugar said, "That white boy is off the chain, ain't he?" She laughed as Tony opened the door to his ride for her in.

"Yeah he is." Tony smiled as he closed her door. "I've been telling that cracker to tone that shit down before he get caught up, but he's young. He was elected to congress when he was 25 and you can't tell him shit. I met him in Afghanistan and took him under my wing. He's good people though."

"Yeah, he seems like it. But he sure is wild as fuck."

"No doubt." Stopping to look at her, Tony smiled and said, "Sugar, I got somewhere I want to take you. The night is still young and it's such a beautiful evening with that full moon out and all. You down?"

"Sure, Mr. Stallworth. I'm down." Moments later, Tony's Mustang pulled over alongside of the road and they exited. Holding hands they crossed over the sand dunes to the Jacob Riis Park on the beach and began walking along the water's edge. As the foamy waves crashed into the shore, making a crackling sound with each surge inland, the faint crooning of seagulls could be heard in the distance, and the strong smell of the salty ocean mist totally permeated the night air. Still walking aimlessly hand and hand along the shore, Tony broke the silence.

"Sugar, where do you see yourself in ten years?" Sugar smiled. The question kinda caught her off guard. However, Tony's straight to the point attitude was a turn-on for her.

"Hmmmm, let's seeee. In ten years...A mother, and maybe a wife. If I'm married, an accountant over my husband's business." Tony smiled as they continued to walk.

"A wife and mother, huh? A mother of how many kids?"

"Oh about three or four, maybe more."

"Is that riiiight?" Tony said smiling. *A woman who knows what she wants in life. I dig that,* he thought.

"Yep! That's right. Three or four, maybe more."

"Sounds like your husband will have his work cut out for him."

"He sure will." She chuckled. "Okay now, Mr. Stallworth. Where do you see yourself in ten years?"

"Ten years from now? Let's seeeee. Perhaps married to an accountant with about three or four kids, maybe more."

"Okay, Mr. Stallworth," she said with a cynical smile. "I hear you talking." When it came to men, Sugar didn't trust easily. But something about this man seemed totally different. His charm and demeanor totally disarmed her. She felt safe with him and around him.

Tony suddenly stopped dead in his tracks and turned to face her, still holding her hand, then said in a serious voice.

"Do you *really* hear me, Miss Jones?"

Sugar's eyes were locked on his without blinking when she said in an equally serious tone, "Don't play with me, Tony. I'm not a play thing."

"I don't play games, Miss Jones," he said before placing a gentle kiss on her lips that quickly graduated into a full blown kiss. Without saying another word, and communicating through lover's telepathy, they made their way to the car before heading back to Tony's crib. Shortly after arriving, Tony put on some love ballads before he and Sugar resumed where they left off while on the beach, while the song *Tonight* by John Legend featuring Ludacris played from the stereo. Following a few moments of slow, passionate kisses, Tony pulled Sugar's blouse over her head and removed her bra revealing her beautiful, hand sized breasts. Her nipples were full, firm, and protruding as a result of the sudden rush of blood and adrenaline coursing through her veins. As she stood there in front of him in a trance-like state, and seemingly receptive to what was taking place, Tony advanced on her, gently running his tongue in a circular motion over her jutted out nipples. When she began to pant and moan and as her breathing became labored, Tony methodically made his way to her perfectly round belly button causing her to momentarily halt his seductive onslaught.

"Don't hurt me, Tony, I'm fragile." she said in a low gasp as her heart continued to pound rapidly.

With his eyes locked into place on hers, he said, "I would never, ever hurt you, babygirl."

She shook her head slowly then placed her fingers on his lips. "I'm talking about my heart, Tony."

"Like I said, I would never, ever hurt you." With those words of assurance, Sugar fully submitted her heart and her body to him that night as he commenced kissing her belly button, surrounded by a well-sculpted six pack. After going as far as he could before running into the last obstacle of clothing, Tony unzipped her skirt, removed her thong and gently laid her down on his satin sheets, while slowly kissing her pelvic area, soliciting more heavy breathing with every movement of his moist tongue. Finally making his way to the grand prize with his tongue, Sugar's body began to convulse as her eyes rolled into the back of her skull, and her hips thrust forward in a constant, rhythmic motion.

Once Tony finished teasing her well stimulated clit with some extended foreplay, he slowly mounted her, kissing her gently on her neck while making deep incursions inside of her as the song *I Do Love You* by GQ played. For the next couple of hours, with brief intermissions in the action, Tony and Sugar continued to consummate their relationship by switching and rotating positions as their bodies exchanged climaxes. For the first time, and after at least three months of dating, Tony had finally penetrated Sugar's emotional guards as well as her pussy. So now, without a doubt, he knew she was his woman. But then again, he knew from the very first time he conversed with her, she would be his woman.

CATO

Chapter 16

Meeting of the Minds

The next evening at six, an hour and a half before the scheduled meeting with Nathan Ward and the other disgruntled O.G. cats, Tony sat inside the Calypso waiting for Genie while the song *War Ready* by Rick Ross, featuring Jeezy, played in the background.

"What's up, Genie?" Tony said as Genie strolled in. "Oh, it ain't nothin,' T. Those O.G. niggas should be here as scheduled."

"Genie, I sure hope that we can get through to those cats."

"Yeah, I hope so too."

"Well, bro, what did you do last night? I dropped by your crib about nine to see if you wanted to go the strip club, but you were gone."

"Yeah, I hung out with my folks last night at that penthouse party."

"Oh yeah? You talking about the one that wild ass politician white boy Josh threw?"

"Yeah that one." Tony laughed. "You know that fool introduced me to the D.A.?" Tony said with a frown on his face. "But he said he was on our team and be snorting up our product."

"T, man, that cracker right there will get a nigga fucked up."

"Nah, he good. I keep him close to me just in case we may need him one day."

"I hear ya, bruh." Genie downed his drink. Genie looked at him momentarily, steady analyzing him."Now to this broad you been kicking it with strong for the past few months." Genie said smiling, "You sound as if this is the one."

"Maybe so, bruh. Maybe so. And you will get to meet her real soon."

At exactly seven sharp, Natty Boy Ward, Cat Eyes Jones, Dallas McNeil, and Jo Jo Carmichael all walked into the Calypso as Tony greeted them at the door.

"Gentlemen! How are you tonight? Glad you could make it." True to his belligerent, straight-forward self, Cat Eye Jones responded in a contemptuous tone.

"We doin' alright, but not half as good as you! In fact, if I had just one of your hands, I would cut off both of mine." Tony smirked and looked over at Genie as he shook the O.G.'s hands. Genie was totally un-amused and didn't even attempt to hide it.

"Have a seat, gentlemen. Can I get any of you something to drink?"

"Yeah sure, Tony, we could use some drinks," Natty Boy said. Tony then summoned for the waitress. "Well, gentlemen, I'm going to get right down to the business of this meeting. I've been hearing that you cats aren't too happy about the current state of the streets nowadays. And so my question to you is, why is that? Because without a doubt, gentlemen, you have it better now than you did when you were plugged in with Mr. Rios."

Natty Boy paused momentarily before answering as the waitress served their drinks. "Thank you, baby," he said to her. Natty Boy took a sip before responding. "Well, Tony, as I'm sure you are aware, my associates and me have been running this city and doing our thing for well over forty years with a few problems here and there, we eventually prevailed on, and with very little competition. We were here during the time of Frank Lucas and Nicky Barnes and we were still going strong. But lately, something unprecedented has taken place on our turf, right here in the place we call home. Lately, we've been in competition with the up and comers. Young niggas who's getting a price so low, they don't have to come to us anymore. Cats who just a couple of weeks ago, did business with us, but with your arrival that may be a thing of the past, and this is a concern for us. We are simply too old to be competing."

Jo Jo Carmichael interjected. "Tony, what Nathan here is trying to say, with all due respect is, you're stepping on our toes a little."

Cat Eye Jones shook his head, waved his hands in the air and said after downing his drink, "Sheeiit! Not just a little, JoJo! Mr. Stallworth done practically broke my damn foot he's stepped on it so hard!

Tony paused for a second before responding. "Well, gentlemen, I didn't realize you all been having such a hard time lately." He then cut his eye over at Genie, whose facial expression clearly verbalized his thoughts, fuck'em! "So what do you gentlemen recommend or have in mind to make things better for yourselves? Because the last thing I want to do is cause any of you any hardships. I have mad respect for each and every one of you. Besides all that, as black men who have chosen the underworld to make our living, we should stand united for this cause and do whatever it takes to keep the peace, and make a fortune doing it. Because gentlemen, it goes without saying none of this shit is legal."

Natty Boy, the diplomat of the bunch, answered with a smile. "Tony, we think it would be a great help to us all if you lowered the price a few points on our end to allow us to get things back under control, so to speak." Tony's eyes then shifted to the other three O.G.s.

"Well, gentlemen, will this make things better between us?" They all looked at each other and nodded in approval, all except Cat Eye who was never known for his diplomacy. Nevertheless, Tony respected him the most because of his straightforwardness. Cat Eye was an associate of his Uncle Walt, and with an O.G. like old Cat Eye, what you see is what you get.

"Hold on. Before we say that all is well, fellas, what kinda price is Mr. Stallworth talking? And not only that, will he guarantee us that his people, who I'm sure will be getting a similar price, or maybe even better, won't continue to 'step on our toes' as Jo Jo here put it?"

Tony looked over at Genie and quickly waved him off just as he was about to snap.

"Okay gentlemen. I will drop the price to let's saaaaay, five points to fifteen a key for you and you only. And as for my people stepping on your toes, that shouldn't happen anymore because that puts you two points lower than what they get it for. So, gentlemen, with this new arrangement, this should put you all back in control of things. But now it's going to be up to you to maintain that control, because I won't stop my people from putting down on the street, you dig? Besides, fellas, we live in a free market economy where competition is good for business. As those big wheels on Wall Street say, "competition is the American way."

With that said, Tony stood up as did the O.G.s. "We have no problem with that, Tony," Natty Boy said as he shook his hand. "I think that's very generous on your part." The other O.G.s also shook Tony's hand before exiting the Calypso. Genie looked over at Tony with a look of utter contempt on his face. After quickly downing his drink, Genie finally exploded.

"Ain't that a bitch, man! Them whiny, outdated, ungrateful ass niggas! Bruh, I really think you bent too much on that one. If it was me? I'd say fuck'em!"

"Look, Genie." Tony placed his hand on his shoulder. "I know they some whiney, ungrateful ass muthafuckas. But I did this to keep from having to murder them, bruh. I'm just trying to keep the peace and run our thing as smoothly as possible, you dig? Remember why we're in this shit. We in it to win it and make money and nothing else." Genie nodded his head.

"Okay, T, I hope you on point with this one. But you know better than me how these things normally go. We will have to end up murdering them niggas anyway."

"Well, I hope you're wrong, Genie," Tony said as he patted his partner on his back. "But keeping it gutter with you, I have that same feeling too."

After climbing into the pearl white caddy limo with gangster white walls, and pulling off from the curb in front of the Calypso, flanked by their soldiers in two other vehicles, Natty Boy took a sip from a solid gold flask and sat there silent.

"Well, Nathan, what do you really think about the new arrangement with Stallworth?" Dallas McNeil asked, sitting across from him. After firing up a cigar and taking a couple of tokes from it, he answered with humility.

"I happen to think it was a good deal, Dallas. What do you think?"

"Well yeah, Nathan, I happen to think so too." Natty Boy looked over at Cat Eye.

"What about you, Cat Eye?" he asked in a cynical tone. "You think Stallworth gave us a good deal?" Cat Eye smirked then took a sip from his pearl white and chrome flask and answered in classic Cat Eye Jones fashion.

"Sheeeiiit! Ain't no deal a good deal unless that deal keep us in control of the shit we built for the past forty years!"

"Well, Cat Eye, I think the new arrangement did just that," Natty Boy said. "You heard what Stallworth said. He dropped the price a few points for us."

"Yeah, Nathan, I know that's what the nigga said. But how do we know he'll keep his word?" Natty Boy removed his cigar from his mouth.

"All a man has is his word, Cat Eye. And I happen to believe that Stallworth is a stand up cat."

"Okay, Nathan, maybe he is. But are you willing to stake all that we've built on it? I know I'm not! You Jo Jo?" Jo Jo shook his head. "What about you, Dallas?" He too shook his head joining the naysayers. "Ummm hmmm. Yeah. That's what I thought." Cat Eye said confidently before taking another sip from his flask. "You know, when I was at home the other day lounging around the house, I watched that animal show, Wild Kingdom. You know the show that old shriveled up honkie Marlin Perkins be on? Well, there was this group of bitch lions over in Africa they call a Pride, ruled by this huge older male lion who had nuts bigger than all ours put together. The muthafucka wasn't nothing but an old pimp," he said as everybody laughed. "Anyway, after his bitches took down this big ass Wildebeest and sat down to feast, with him getting his share of the kill first, of course, even though that muthafucka sat up under some tree in the shade while all the killing was going on, he heard a roar and caught the scent of another male trespassing on his territory, causing him to venture out and investigate. After about a couple of miles of following the scent and the distinct roars that signaled a challenge to his authority, he stumbled upon two young male lions on his turf standing there about a hundred yards away glaring at him with that unmistakable look of ambition and determination in their eyes. Accepting the challenge head on, the elder lion did exactly what he had done for years to protect his family and turf. He attacked his rivals, but let up on them after they retreated. So thinking there was no more threat from the ambitious youngsters, he returned home to his pride of bitches, confident that the shit was over with. However, the very next day the youngsters returned as bold as ever with that same look of ambition in their eyes, but this time the look was more intense." Cat Eye paused momentarily to take another sip from his flask.

"Well?" Jo Jo asked anxiously. "What happened next, Cat Eye?"

Cat Eye fired up a cigar, took a drag from it then answered, "After the young lions whupped his muthafuckin' ass and ran him off the turf he controlled ever since he had took it from some other muthafucka, he lost his bitches, his cubs, and he eventually lost his life when some other lions caught him all alone one day with no more protection and wasted his ass, leaving his carcass for them damn hyenas. So I said all that shit to say this! I'm an old lion with big nuts, and I ain't lettin' no ambitious youngster come and take over some shit I been running for the past twenty-five years!" With that said, all of the O.G.s nodded their heads in agreement as the white caddy limo turned onto Fulton Street, with its stereo playing *Walk On By* by Isaac Hayes.

CATO

Chapter 17

Hail to the King

Over the next several months, Tony further tightened his yoke on the five boroughs, the tri-states, and in other distribution points that now penetrated into the Carolina's and parts of Maryland. With steady shipments of two thousand bricks a month, Tony's ever increasing customer base now included certain Italian Mafia families in New York and Jersey, who although resented the idea of coping dope from a *Moolie,* couldn't resist the chance of enriching themselves. However, while Tony's organization raked in millions, the state of the streets for the time being was all good. The best way to characterize this situation on the streets is, it was as if the streets of Brooklyn was raining gold, or at least raining a substance worth its weight in gold here, in the western hemisphere.

Tony's sudden rise to power and prominence gave him something more valuable than money. It gave him political connections that enabled him to rub elbows with Mayors, City Councilmen, and even clergy while greasing the palms of certain prosecutors, police chiefs, and other high ranking pigs, rendering him virtually untouchable. And this was all made possible by the almighty dollar and America's insatiable appetite for dope, which was by far, the most narcotized nation on the face of the earth, receiving and consuming at least ninety percent of all coke imports to the western hemisphere.

Antonio Stallworth who, just like any other up and coming gangster who seemed to have solved the complex nature of the streets to extract gold from it, was a homegrown byproduct of America's incessant desire to stay fucked up.

Billed as Sugar's graduation celebration from accountant school, but in reality a celebration of Tony's success, he threw a huge bash at the Calypso that included a star studded showcase of R-Kelly, Charlie Wilson, Ciara, Rick Ross, and Rihanna. At the celebration, Tony and Sugar, and Genie and his girl, Selina, accompanied by their organization, and their respective women all filed out of their gangster rides that ranged from Maybachs and Bentleys, Rolls Royces to Limos and tricked out Escalades. The scene outside of the Calypso was reminiscent of the pomp and spectacle you would witness at a celebrity funeral procession. Before Tony's entourage could even reach the front entrance of the club, which was lined with security, the deafening sound of the music immediately hit them in their faces. The bass from the speakers were so loud that it could damn near cause a coronary. Once inside, they found the huge club packed with wall to wall patrons and an entire section reserved especially for them.

The club's DJ, Tracy T, gave Tony and his entourage a shout out as they all filed in.

"Ladies and gentlemen! Pimps, hoes, killers and gangsters alike! Recogniiiize! Mr. Antonio Stallworth, Genie Boy Smalls, and family! Flanked by the soldiers, Tony and Sugar walked arm-in-arm like heads of state followed by their organization.

Tony, whose hands were smothered down in ice, wore a white mink coat with a burgundy suit on underneath, and a gangster lid to match, accented with a white, black, and burgundy feather. Covering his wheels were burgundy and black gators accented with gold clamps. Sugar, who looked just as immaculate as her king, her hands and neck were smothered down in diamonds and rubies, and her body draped in a white Chinchilla coat that came slightly above her waist. Underneath, she wore a long, platinum, satin sequin dress with a split that slightly revealed one of her pecan tan thighs. Genie, his woman, and the rest of the entourage were sharp as hell also, wearing the latest in gangster fashions, and everyone's eyes were fixated on them. Some with the look of respect and admiration and others with the unmistakable looks of jealousy and envy. But whatever the reasons behind the many long stares, it was obvious to all those who were present, who the real main attraction was this night.

After Tony's folks sat down at their tables, and just before the first group took to the stage, the who's who of the tri-states gangster world made their way over to Tony to pay their respects. Or in other words, do some serious ass kissing. Nathan Ward, Cat Eye Jones, Dallas McNeil, and Jo Jo Carmichael, and a few up and coming hustlers all dropped by to kiss the ring. After they all finished paying their respects, and walked away, Genie leaned over and said to Tony with disdain, "Ole fake ass niggas!" Tony smiled and nodded his head.

Moments later, DJ Tracy T came over the mike and announced the first group of the evening.

"Ladies and gentlemen! This is the moment you've all been waiting for. I introduce to you, Rihanna!" Her opening song was *Bitch Better Have My Money,* which brought the women to their feet. The women in the crowd all swayed back and forth in their seats like hypnotized cobras, and the men sat there leaning in cool ass gangster poses with a black and mild in one hand, and a drink in the other, as the music bounced off the walls, giving everybody present a collective melodic high. The atmosphere in the Calypso was reminiscent of that scene on the movie *The Mack* where Goldie and his bitches were at the pimps' ball. And a ball it was. A gangster's ball. Every Gangster or hustler worth the name, including the contenders and wannabes, tried to look impressive, all for the sake of the many square ass niggas and broads present. If a cat wanted to be seen and recognized as gangster, this was definitely the stage to be seen on, because this was one of those rare opportunities of a lifetime for maximum exposure, other than a newspaper write up of a drug bust.

Following the fine ass Rihanna, one by one each entertainer came on stage and put on a memorable performance as the celebration marking Tony's success went on nonstop into the wee hours of the morning. At around 3 a.m., when the once packed Calypso began to empty out, Tony and Sugar, accompanied by Genie and his girl, Selina, left the club without his security and headed to Daisy's Diner on Fifth Avenue in Park Slope. On the way there, the car was filled with laughter and animated conversation concerning the night's events at the Calypso. The only one in the car not taking part in the jovial chatter was Tony, who was preoccupied with the two vehicles that had been trailing them from the moment they left the Calypso. Not wanting to frighten Sugar and Selina, he tapped Genie who was napping, and calmly nodded to the pair of cars trailing them. Still groggy and feeling the effects of the multiple shots of Crown Royal, Genie peered into the mirror and saw the two ominous looking rides methodically hanging in behind them about three cars back.

"How long they been behind us, T?" Genie asked, now suddenly sober and wide awake.

"Not long after we pulled off from the Calypso," Tony answered in a whisper. Genie's face immediately showed concern. "Hey Genie," Tony said with his eyes locked in on the two vehicles. "Just in case something goes down, get your tool on point."

Not saying another word, he and Genie simultaneously eased out their pistols from the holsters and placed them in their laps then flipped them off the safety. Meanwhile, Sugar and Selina continued on laughing and talking, totally oblivious to the imminent danger creeping ominously behind them. With his eyes still super-glued to the mirror, and calmly driving only five miles per hour over the speed limit, Tony whispered to Genie, "I'm gonna hit a couple of blocks to see if these niggas continue to tag along behind us."

After hitting a couple of blocks, then veering onto the street leading back to the main intersection, Tony knew that something was about to go down as the two vehicles began closing the gap while he pulled up to the red light.

"Hey Genie, I have a feeling that when this light change, shortly thereafter all hell is going to break loose, bruh." Genie nodded, and tightly clutched his pistols without saying a word. Tony then calmly interrupted the two women who still had no idea as to what was about to take place.

"Hey, babygirl! I need for you and Selina to get all the way down in the floorboard, okay?"

"Tony, what's going on, baby?" Sugar asked with a concerned look on her face.

"Look, babygirl, y'all just do what I say and get down in the floorboard!"

Without any further inquiry, the two women obeyed and immediately slid down in the floorboard to take cover. Their hearts were racing. Tony then placed his hand on one of his nickel plated .45s and started tapping on it with his fingertips with anticipation as he stared at the two vehicles behind them. From his observations, he could see there were four cats in each vehicle, mean mugging, and glaring directly at them with *murder, murder, murder* written all over their faces. *This shit is going to get ugly,* he thought to himself.

"Hey, Genie, as soon as the light turn green, I'm going to punch it, bro. So be ready to cut loose on them."

"Okay, T."

While the light remained red, the three lone vehicles just sat there poised for the next turn of events to transpire. One vehicle's occupants looking to preserve life, or at least the lives of their own. And the occupants of the other two vehicles behind them, obviously commissioned by some unknown source or sources, looking to take their lives. However, the intended target was

Tony, and he figured this much. Everyone else would just be collateral damage. But what Tony saw on those cats' faces, everybody along with him had to die this night if they had it their way. Seconds later, for what seemed like an eternity, the light finally turned green and Tony immediately floored the Bentley, causing the engine to moan, veering right and cutting off the car directly behind him. When the two vehicles quickly recovered, they followed in behind him in hot pursuit, with their engines howling.

Zig-zagging from side to side, Tony quickly maneuvered his vehicle to prevent the assassins from pulling alongside of them. As Tony continued down the near empty city streets, one of the vehicles managed to pull up alongside of him and got off a couple of shots shattering Genie's window. Genie responded by sticking his guns out of the shattered window and returning fire while Tony kept the vehicle on his side at bay.

"Here babygirl," Tony said to Sugar, throwing her his mink coat so she and the hysterical Selina could shield themselves from the broken shards of glass and debris that rained down on them. The deafening blasts of gunfire sounded like a war zone as the three vehicles darted through the near empty city streets. While Genie continued to exchange fire with the black SUV on his side, causing it to swerve from side to side, Tony drove fast and furiously, staying ahead of the other SUV on his side, topping speeds of 100 miles an hour.

"Hey, Genie, I'm going to try something!" Tony said, steering the Bentley. "When I hit this sudden turn in the middle of the road, I want you to cut loose on the car on your side, okay Genie?"

"Alright, T, man I'm ready!" Genie replied as he remained crouched down low in his seat waiting for the right moment to spring up and rain on them. Tony proceeded to drive on about a five hundred yards ahead then suddenly hit the brakes causing the Bentley's occupants bodies to slam forward. Swerving to his right, he forced the vehicle on his right side to slow down to a near screeching halt.

"*Now Genie!*" Tony yelled. Genie then popped up like a jack-in-the-box with his two burners blazing, unleashing a deadly hail of lead poison on the SUV on his side, shattering the windshield and killing the driver instantly. The dead driver's foot stomped down on the gas causing the vehicle to pick up speed and bolt off the highway out of control before hitting a parked car then flipping several times into the glass window of a storefront and catching fire. The explosion could be heard in the distance as the assassins in the remaining vehicle continued pursuing Tony's Bentley, hanging out of their windows firing relentlessly as he swerved from east to west in an attempt to avoid the flying projectiles.

"Genie, how are you on ammo?" Genie examined his last magazine.

"I'm down to three shots, T. What about you?"

"I'm down to about four," he said as he jumped off the highway, hitting block after block and momentarily losing the hitters.

"Sugar, y'all alright back there?" Tony asked.

"Yeah, we're okay, Tony," she said as she continued to hold the once hysterical Selina who had become eerily quiet at this point, perhaps from shock. Just as Tony slowed down thinking that he had lost them for good, suddenly out of nowhere the killers' vehicle boned around the corner with its occupants hanging out of their windows blasting. Tony responded by sticking his .45 out of his window and firing backwards as he punched the gas with the carload of goons dead on his trail. In a deadly game of cat and mouse, the two vehicles blazed through the ghetto streets with their car engines howling. The sparks that flickered underneath the bottom of their rides every time it came into contact with the concrete along with the intermittent flames that jutted forth from the barrels of their guns, provided a beautiful, but deadly, light show in the near complete darkness of the hood streets during the wee hours of the morning. Tony continued to navigate his bullet riddled Bentley with expert precision, fishtailing and plowing down stop signs.

Genie, meanwhile, finally got an angle on the SUV and squeezed off a couple more shots hitting it and forcing the killers to slow down. This gave Tony enough room to lose them once again as he dipped in and out and hitting block after block with his eyes still glued to the rear view mirror looking for signs of the killers. Sensing that he may have lost them for good this time, but not wanting to take any chances, Tony pulled in behind some of the abandoned row houses out of sight then quickly cut his lights and engine.

"Genie, I think we lost them for good this time," Tony said as he continued to look around.

"I hope so, because I'm all out of ammo now."

Tony examined his own clip. "I'm down to two myself." Suddenly, as Tony's ears caught the loud, distinct sound of the Hummer's engine driven by the killers, he motioned for everyone to be quiet.

"Shhhhh!" he said with his .45 in front of his face. As the vehicle slowly crept by, the killers' heads were hanging out of both sides of the windows rotating back and forth as if their heads were on swivels, steadily trying to locate their quarry. They could be heard loud and clear levying profanities.

"Damn! Shit! Them muthafuckas done got away, man! Y'all see them niggas?"

"Nah man. No sign of'em," one of them said. "Fuck!" The killers' curses and the noise from their vehicle's engine were the only sounds that could be heard. However, those sounds soon began to get farther and farther away as the blare of sirens in the distance started to replace it. Moments later, the long wail of the sirens were now the only sound that could be heard in what was left of the night. After remaining frozen for the past ten minutes, and not making a sound, Tony broke the silence.

"I think they're gone now, Genie," he whispered. "But to make sure, I'm gonna go take a look. Be back in a minute," he said as he slipped out of the Bentley and ran in a crouch to the edge of the road to make sure the killers had ghost the scene. Not seeing or hearing anything other than the approaching sirens inching ever closer, he was now confident that the killers were finally gone. He then bolted back to the car and quickly fired up the engine.

"They're gone now!" he said as he slowly inched the Bentley forward ever so slightly. Seeing that the coast was clear, he cautiously pulled from behind the abandoned houses with the lights still off then floored the Bentley, causing the engine to let out a deafening roar, leaving a cloud of gravel and sand in his aftermath. Within minutes, Tony pulled on the front lawn of Genie's crib with the lights off, and immediately after the war torn Bentley's tires came to a sudden halt, digging up patches of grass, he and Genie jumped out with their pistols drawn and crouching low in a defensive posture just in case the assassins doubled back. After backing up to his crib, Genie quickly opened his front door so Tony could usher Sugar and the petrified Selina inside. Genie then cautiously backed inside with his pistols still drawn looking up the block. Once inside, Sugar immediately led Selina to the back bedroom to continue calming her down, while Genie stood at the living room window peeping out of the blinds like a paranoid crack head.

"Hey Genie, call the Professor and the muscle and tell them to get here, *now!*" Without saying a word, Genie pulled out his cell and made the call while Tony headed to the back to check on the girls. When he entered, Sugar looked up at him with a concerned look as she cradled Selina in her arms.

"Babygirl, are y'all alright?" he asked as he sat down on the bed beside her and began brushing the fine shards of broken glass from her head.

"Yeah, we're good. Selina is just a little shaken up, but she'll be okay though."

"Hey, T, they're on their way," Genie said as he sat down and started consoling his woman. Within minutes, the sound of screeching tires, slamming doors and the hard soles of dress shoes and boots tapping against the concrete could be heard outside. The Professor, Macky Boy, and the muscle who were still dressed in the suits they wore to the club, all quickly filed out of their vehicles armed with pistols, pump shotguns, and automatic assault rifles. Under Macky Boy's command, the muscle scrambled up to the house's perimeter to provide a phalanx of security while the Professor rushed up to the front door where Genie was standing.

"Is everyone alright, Genie? What the fuck happened?" the Professor asked.

"Yeah everybody alright. Some clowns tried to murk us shortly after we left the Calypso, but they fucked it up."

"Well, where's Tony?"

"He's in the back with the girls," Genie answered as he poured him a stiff drink.

"Everybody okay?" Macky Boy asked, rushing in.

"Yeah, they alright," the Professor said. "You have any idea who was behind this, Genie?" the Professor asked.

"Nah not as of right now, but you can put it on everything we will eventually!" Genie said as Tony emerged entering the living room.

"Like Genie said, we will find out who commissioned those rank amateurs tonight." Tony's dress shirt and holsters were still covered with shards of glass and his two .45s were still hot from the gun battle. He then dropped down on the couch, wearing a dangerous look on his face. "Okay Professor. This is what I want you to do. I don't want any business done in this city. Not even a single gram of coke, you feel me? *Nothing* is to be sold in this city until we find out who was responsible for this shit tonight. An extended drought will make muthafuckas suffer because they can't eat. And when muthafuckas can't eat because of shit someone else did, someone will come forward and start IDing folks!"

"Okay, Tony, consider it done," the Professor said. Before walking out, he nodded to Genie, and touched Tony on the shoulder. "We'll find'em, Tony," he said before exiting the house.

The young lieutenant, Macky Boy, also made his own vow before leaving. "Yeah, Mr. Stallworth. We'll find those muthafuckas and I will deal with them *personally!* You have my word on that, sir."

Tony nodded his head as he looked off into space as if he were mentally incarcerated in some sort of maniacal dream. Tonight's near tragic events set a very serious precedent in Tony's life. For the first time, with the exception of his stint in Afghanistan, he had become the prey instead of the predator. But in his mind he always knew that this possibility existed, because that shit came with the game. However, the thing he never fathomed, or calculated as a risk in his former or current profession, was that someone he loved dearly, a civilian, a non-combatant, his woman, would become a target directly or indirectly, purposely, or un-purposely. Nevertheless this shit happened. The strict boundaries that Tony had set for himself and lived by ever since he embarked on a trade in which he was a well-paid, well sought after assassin, had just been transgressed by some unknown source or sources, for some unknown reason. But whoever the source, and for whatever their motivation, the shit didn't matter. There was definitely going to be a reckoning. On his mother, father, and uncle there was definitely going to be a reckoning. Because for only the second time in his life, this shit was personal!

CATO

Chapter 18

A Real Trooper for a Woman

Later that evening after recovering from both mental and physical exhaustion of last night's events, Tony and Sugar finally awakened from their slumber. Deeply troubled about what happened and putting Sugar in harm's way, Tony began to profusely apologize the moment he woke up.

"Babygirl look!" he said as he turned over to face her. "I am so sorry about what happened this morning. I never intended for you, never in my wildest nightmares did I ever intend for you to ever get caught up in my shit."

"Tony," she said, placing her hand gently on his face. "You don't have to keep apologizing for something you had no control over."

"Yeah, babygirl, but I've always ensured that no one close to me ever became a caught up in my shit. And I feel like I let you down by bringing you into something you shouldn't have been introduced to. I should have at least brought along some security," he said with his head down.

"Tony, you don't think I know who and what I'm involved with? I knew after that night outside the club, since that time and up until now, that the man I fell in love with is a gangster. So no matter what, I'm going to remain at my man's side through thick and thin, you dig?" Tony smiled and placed a soft kiss on her lips.

"Babygirl, you are one of a kind."

"Of course I am," she said smiling. "I'm project raised, remember? I came up around the gangster shit."

"Oh, so you mean to tell me you weren't scared this morning just a little?" he said laughing.

"Me, scared? A project chick like me?" Some much needed laughter filled the room. However, they both knew that what happened last night was some serious shit that could not be repeated. Nonetheless, Tony was extremely impressed and amazed at not only the calm and resilience Sugar displayed under fire, but how she was able to handle things after the fact by bringing laughter to some shit that was by no means a laughing matter. For this woman to still be laying by his side after two car loads of killers nearly wasted them only hours earlier, further convinced him that he had a real trooper for a woman.

Chapter 19

A Declaration of War

Two weeks after the assassination attempt and the subsequent self-imposed drought that put a virtual stranglehold on the city and surrounding cities, Tony summoned his organization to an emergency meeting in the huge conference room in the rear of one of his grocery stores in the hood, which would be the site for all future meetings. At the conference room's roundtable, Tony and Genie sat as the members all filed in and took their places, while the soldiers with dark shades on stood with their backs against the wall.

For those like Genie who truly knew Tony, recognized the various moods Tony could be in, but this one was different. This mood was one Genie had never seen before. Tony stood up and began pacing in front of his men when he started to speak.

"Okay. As all of you are already aware of by now, there was an attempt a couple weeks ago on my life, that of my woman, and that of Genie and his woman. This is the major reason why I called this meeting here today. Macky Boy here was informed by one of the hitters just before he died, that Nathan "Natty Boy" Ward commissioned him and others to carry out that very ama-teurish hit, which they obviously fucked up, because I'm still here," he said with his voice rising. "Also, we can't leave out the other syndicate cats. They were all complicit. So therefore, I want all of them hit! Mr. Cat Eye Jones, Jo Jo Carmichael and Dallas McNeil, I want them hit! In fact, all those associated with each and every one of them, which includes Mr. Ward, I want them muthafuckas hit too! From their muscle, on down to their push-ers, I want them hit, you dig? I want them and their organizations wiped off the face of this earth where there's not even a trace, as if they never even existed! However, *don't* touch one strand of nappy hair on Mr. Ward's head! I repeat! Do not touch one hair on Mr. Ward's head, you feel me? I want his ass alive, conscious, in one piece and with all the feeling still left in his body when I pay his ass a visit! Is this understood, gentlemen?"

Everyone nodded without saying a word, and there was no need to. The situation, the tone, the body language was obvious, and spoke for itself. War had just been officially declared.

"Okay gentlemen, this meeting is adjourned," Tony said before all of the members, with the exception of the Professor and Macky Boy, quietly filed out after receiving their marching orders.

"Okay, Professor, go ahead and lift the drought and resume operations, but only to those hustlers not affiliated with the syndicate cats." The Professor nodded his head and exited the conference room. "Okay youngster, here is where you show me what you're made of. It's real nigga time," Tony said, looking Macky Boy straight in his eyes. But I want you to take all security measures and make absolutely sure that no civilians get caught up in this, okay?"

"Yes sir, Mr. Stallworth. I won't let you down," he said before exiting the room.

Genie grabbed his partner's shoulder and said, "T, man, this shit is going to get ugly, but we will see it through."

Tony just stood there silent, leaning against the podium with a menacing look on his face as Genie walked out of the conference room.

Chapter 20

I'm Cat Eye Muthafuckin' Jones

Laying low in one of his many secret hideouts after the failed assassination attempt on Tony, Cat Eyes Jones sipped on some Martel as he waited for the trick bitch, Blossom, to emerge from the bathroom. Cat Eye was her high paying regular who she once considered being his side bitch, but she couldn't stand the idea of being controlled, which is why she no longer had a pimp. Besides, in her mind, Cat Eye broke big bread with her every week, and sometimes twice a week, like clockwork, so there was no need to be his side piece. It was well known that Cat Eye was a legendary trick, although he'd been married to the same woman for well over thirty years.

"Hey Blossom! What the hell takin' you so long, baby? Whatchu doin' in there?"

"I'll be out in a minute, Cat Eye," she answered as she took a quick look at her watch while freshening up her money maker. As the song *Lady Marmalade* by Patti LaBelle played on the radio, Cat Eye sipped on his cognac feeling defiant and thinking to himself, *That young wet nosed punk Stallworth got some fuckin' nerve thinkin' he can just show up outta nowhere and take over some shit we been running before his pappy squirted him in his mammy's pussy! Sheeiiid! I'm Cat Eye muthafuckin' Jones! And ain't no sucker gone control me!*

Cat Eye then poured himself another drink as the Martel steadily increased his defiance with every round. *Yeah, that muthafucka lucked up and got away this time, but we never miss twice. We'll off the young punk sooner or later.*

"Blossom! What the fuck takin' you so long, bitch? I ain't got no time to be waitin' on yo ass all night!"

"I'm coming, Cat Eye baby, just a minute," she said as she looked at her watch again. The time was 8:50pm and the young handsome cat who paid her five stacks up front a couple days ago to set up a private meeting with Cat Eye, assured her he would be there at nine sharp and give her another five more stacks shortly after he arrived. For over five years, she had been tricking with Cat Eye and had even developed an affinity for him, not to mention her appreciation for the bread she'd made off him over that time period. That's what made her feel a slight degree of guilt for what she had done, but that feeling of guilt evaporated from her conscience faster than the nut Cat Eye busted every time single time he stuck his dick in her.

The ten thousand dollar payoff and the street law of self-preservation, overruled all other feelings of guilt, compassion or thoughts of betrayal. The talk on the streets was, Cat Eye, Natty Boy Ward and their associates days were numbered, but to Blossom whether or not any of that shit was true didn't matter to her, because she wasn't taking any chances. There were also ten thousand reasons why she wasn't taking any chances. Being a street vet, and an outlaw bitch who had been independent for years ever since she set up her pimp for a fee to get murdered, she knew all too well since the tender age of fourteen, when she turned her first trick, that the only thing in life that was certain- always go with the sure payoff.

"You ready for me, daddy? Here I come," she said, taking one last look at the time before she emerged naked from the bathroom. Like always, when she tricked with Cat Eye, she turned off the lights per his request because he said it decreased his guilt of fucking around on his Sunday school teacher wife. Before walking to the bed where Cat Eye lay sprawled with his legs wide open, she unlocked the door without him noticing it.

"*Damn Blossom!* What was you doin' in there, baby? You know I gotta get home to my Naomi."

154

"After all these years, you don't think I know that by now, daddy?" she said, smiling as she sat down beside him and began gently stroking his dick. "Good things come to those who wait, baby," she said before lowering her head between his legs and slowly began running her tongue up and down his dick. As Cat Eyes' eyes rolled in the back of his head from the fire head he was receiving, the front door slowly eased opened and two shadowy figures seeped inside. Noticing them out of the corner of her eyes, Blossom knew this was her cue to ghost the scene and give the two strangers their time alone with Cat Eye.

"You like that, daddy?" she asked in a sensual voice as she continued to bob her head up and down on his curved dick in a rhythmic motion, causing him to moan with his eyes closed, while totally unaware to the treachery unfolding around him. Pausing for a moment from her work, her lips dripping a stream of saliva and pre-cum, Blossom cut her eyes over at the two shadows standing patiently in stealth at the front door.

"Cat Eye, baby, hold on a second, I gotta go pee, honey."

"*What!* Damn Blossom! What's with you tonight? he asked. "You just took forever in there a minute ago."

"I know, daddy," she said, rushing to the bathroom. "But I didn't have to use it then. I'll be right out."

"Okay, Blossom, but don't take too long, 'cause you know my dick can't stay up like it used to." Just before she walked into the bathroom, she nodded to the two shadowy figures standing ominously in the cut. Once inside the bathroom, she quickly gathered her belongings, threw on her clothes and boots, then crept out with her purse slung over her shoulder. Just as she walked over to the two shadows, Cat Eye began calling for her again. "Blossom! What's takin' you so long, girl? I done told you my shit gonna go limp!"

One of the shadows handed her an envelope and she quickly scanned its contents before stuffing it in her bra. Before walking out, in what was perhaps a brief moment of conscience, she turned and took one last look in Cat Eye's direction before she left him and the two men alone in privacy to have their meeting.

"Alright, Blossom. Fuck this shit, bitch! I ain't got time for this bullshit here! I pay you too goddamn good to be dealin' with this kinda shit!" *I ain't got time for this. I gotta get home to my Naomi,* he said, mumbling to himself as he sat up on the side of the bed in the pitch dark room. Still mumbling to himself, Cat reached over to turn on the night light when there was a click and the room lit up, momentarily blinding him.

"Damn!" he said out loud. Once he regained the vision in his aging eyes, almost immediately, his ticker started to race with fear from what he saw standing directly in front of him. It was two men hovering over him grinning from ear to ear like hyenas. One of them was Macky Boy, the young handsome cat Blossom met up with a few days ago to set the wheels of betrayal into motion. Cat Eyes fright-filled, wide-stretched eyes slowly shifted down to the tubular device Macky Boy was slowly screwing to the end of the pistol he held in the other hand. It was at this point Cat Eye knew that trick bitch Blossom had just administered the double cross.

His thoughts then immediately shifted to a dire warning his dear wife Naomi once gave him. *Your tricking and running around with those young whores is going to catch up with you one of these days.* And much to his horror, this was that day. *How could that bitch, Blossom, put me in the cross like this after all these years I been fuckin' with her?* he thought to himself. Just as the smiling Macky Boy slowly raised his tool and took careful aim at his dome, Cat Eye's entire life and long career as a flamboyant original gangster flashed before him. All lost for words, and knowing this was one of those situations he couldn't talk or buy his way out of this shit, and realizing this was the end, Cat

Eye let out a primal, high pitched scream just as the orange flames danced in short bursts from the tip of the silencer.

CATO

Chapter 21

Campaign of Terror

Over the next couple of weeks, Tony's muscle, led by Macky Boy, unleashed a campaign of terror against Natty Boy Ward and his syndicate members. There were drive-bys, car bombings, fire bombings, bludgeonings, beatings, stabbings, shootings, and people not waking up due to their throats being slit. The beleaguered syndicate's turf was in complete and utter chaos in what was the worst violence seen since the '68 riots. For Natty Boy, Jo Jo Carmichael, Dallas McNeil and all those associated with them, there was no safe quarter. As a result of this brutal, relentless onslaught by Tony's muscle, Natty Boy and his syndicate associate's rackets began to quickly dry up.

In fact, the situation had become so untenable for them, they made a pathetic overture for a truce, but Tony wasn't having it. He was totally resolute on sending them to their destruction. So there would be no truce. No ceasefire. No arbitration. No peace treaty, or some negotiated peace settlement. To Tony, the only acceptable terms to end the conflict were the lives of all those involved in the assassination attempt on his life, and the lives of his woman and main man Genie - for the code he lived by and never deviated from was, don't allow an avowed enemy of today, live to be an active enemy of tomorrow.

Meanwhile, as the total destruction of the O.G. cats raged on, Tony purchased a huge palatial mansion equipped with a state of the art security system. This mansion included a huge backyard with an obstacle course, exercise yard, swimming pool, and an indoor sound proof gun range. After moving Sugar in and familiarizing her with the various alarms and security systems and their codes, Tony took her to the gun range and trained her to be proficient with the new chrome .38 caliber snub nose he gave her after the assassination attempt. To Tony's surprise, Sugar became a damn good shot in no time, and could even break down her weapon pretty fast. Tony was definitely doing a thorough job of schooling her on some of the deadly skills that made him a legend in his former trade, and little did he know at the present time, it would come in handy.

Chapter 22

Homecoming

A few days after completely moving into their new crib, Tony and Sugar flew to Orlando to visit her grandmother. The trip to Florida was a sense of excitement for Sugar who hadn't seen her granny in nearly two years. For Tony, it was a much needed getaway from the brutality being waged in the city in his name. When the plane finally landed, sending Tony's heart rate back to normal, he and Sugar grabbed their luggage, leased a rental car from Hertz then headed to her grandmother's crib which was about a twenty minute ride from the airport.

On the way there, Sugar gave Tony a brief tour of greater Orlando, and some of the city's famous landmarks, like Disney World and Universal Studios. For a street cat, no tour of Orlando could be called such without at least a pass by one of the infamous spots like Orange Blossom Trail. While cruising through the OBT, Tony noticed some striking similarities between it and the corners in Brooklyn. The hookers darted off on the side streets to meet their tricks, while their pimps stood off congregating with one another and watching with a keen eye. The dope fiends stood around fiending and plotting on their next high as Po Po circled around the blocks in their squad cars like vultures. After leaving the bustling and energetic OBT, Sugar's excitement began to increase as they reached her old neighborhood where her grandmother lived.

"That's where I used to live right there, Tony," she said smiling. "And that's where I attended elementary school right there. My aunt lives there in that house with the big oak tree in the yard. We used to climb that tree all the time, and I still have the scars and bruises to prove it," she said, chuckling. "Okay, Tony, this is my granny's house right here on the left," she said with excitement. As soon as Tony pulled the Cadillac Seville rental into the driveway and came to a stop, Sugar bolted from it, rushed up to the front door and began ringing the doorbell.

"Who is it?"

"It's me, grandmamma! Your favorite granddaughter!" Sugar said, smiling from ear to ear.

"Oh my Lord! It's my baby!" she said before she swung open the door followed by the screen door. A little sweet old lady with long silver hair, and short in stature appeared with outstretched arms as Sugar collapsed right between them. "My baby!" the little old lady said as she and her granddaughter tearfully embraced while Tony stood there at the edge of the steps smiling. It was a very emotional scene right out of one of those tear-jerking movies where two long, lost loved ones had finally reunited. It was obvious that Sugar's grandmother meant the world to her and seeing this, Tony's mind briefly flashed back to the excitement he felt as a child whenever he visited his own grandmother back in Greenville, Alabama. After a few more emotional moments of hugs and kisses, Sugar turned to Tony and said, "Grandma, this is my boyfriend, Tony."

"Heeeey, baby! Nice to meet you!" she said wrapping her arms around him.

"It's nice to meet you too, ma'am. I've heard so much about you." She released him and stood back to get a better look at him.

"If my baby courting you, you must be treating her like the Queen she is, 'cause I raised her not to settle for anything less." Tony smiled and looked over at Sugar.

"Oh yes, ma'am! And you taught her well, because she wouldn't have it any other way."

"Alright, Grandmamma. You have to watch that one," Sugar said with her hands on her hips. "He's one of those New York City smooth talkers." Tony chuckled, and playfully nudged her.

"Baby, y'all come on in and have a seat. If I knew y'all was comin' I woulda cooked something. Are y'all hungry?"

"Yes ma'am!" Sugar blurted out without hesitation. "I'm staaaaaaarving. I haven't had a good home cooked meal since the last time I was home, grandma."

"Umm umm umm," Granny said shaking her head with hands on her hips. "So you mean to tell me you wasn't eating over at ya Aunt Helen's?"

"Now Grandmamma, you know Aunt Helen didn't inherit you and mamma's cooking skills." Granny laughed.

"No, she sure didn't. She was always runnin' them streets too much to learn how to do anything of a domestic nature. That's probably why she could never keep a man. And you young lady, you had better brush up on your cooking so you can keep this man of yours here well fed."

Tony smiled and cleared his throat. "Umm hmm, and I second that."

"Oh, I got him covered, Grandmamma. He ain't going *nowhere!*"

"I hear you talking, child," Grandmamma said with that granny look on her face. "Well, what y'all want Grandmamma to cook?"

"Oooh, Grandmamma! Can you hook up some fried fish and cheese grits?"

"Grandmamma shole can, baby. Is that all you want?"

"Oooh yeah and some of your fried cornbread and some sweet tea too."

"Grandmamma shole can, baby. I will have it done in no time. I have some fish in here already in the icebox that my friend's husband just caught yesterday." Granny then headed into the kitchen to get started. Tony was thoroughly amused by Sugar's antics.

"You so greedy!" He leaned over and whispered into her ear.

"*So!*" she said, popping her neck before they broke out into laughter.

About a half an hour later, Tony and Sugar were treated to a true southern delicacy. Fried Rainbow Trout, cheese grits, fried cornbread, and sweet tea.

"Ma'am, I have to say thank you for that meal. I hadn't had a meal like that since I went to my granny's house in the country."

"Why you are most welcome, baby. It was Grandmamma's pleasure. I didn't mind at all. Glad you enjoyed it. Did you get enough?"

"Oh yes, ma'am. I'm good," Tony said, lying back on the couch.

"Are you sure? I know that granddaughter of mine can eat another helping," she said, smiling at Sugar.

"Oh yes, ma'am. I'm stuffed."

"There's some homemade pound cake in there I just made yesterday. You think you have room for some?"

"Ohhhh no, ma'am. I can't eat another bite. But I tell you what. As soon as I get some room, I will be getting a slice of that pound cake. It's my favorite cake."

"Well, I tell you one person who still have enough room left for some pound cake," Sugar said before getting up from the table and heading to the kitchen. The room filled with laughter.

"That girl there! I tell you. She can eat you out a house and home, and never gain any weight," she said laughing. "Are you sure you gone be able to foot the grocery bill?" she asked Tony.

"After seeing her get down today, I'm not too sure, ma'am," he said laughing. "I may have to apply for some food stamps." The room again filled with laughter.

"I hear y'all in there talking about me," she yelled from the kitchen as she sliced herself a big hunk of the old fashioned lemon pound cake.

After dinner, Grandmamma broke out the family photo albums, and for the next couple of hours, she and Sugar began reminiscing with Tony about old times and family memories. When the evening had died down, and the tiring effects of the delicious meal and the long flight began to set in, Tony and Sugar retired to her old bedroom which was still as she left it after she went off to college. In Sugar's bedroom there were teddy bears covering the head of her bed, and posters of the Jackson Five, Ciara, L.L. Cool J, Mike Tyson, other famous celebs, R & B artists and groups plastered all over her wall. She even had the posters of Scarface, Al Capone and Lucky Luciano on her wall, much to Tony's amusement. After a hot bath, and collapsing into her bed right before falling asleep, Sugar kissed Tony.

"Thank you, baby, for bringing me home to see my grandmamma."

"And you are welcome, babygirl. In fact, you are more than welcome, you are most deserving." Moments later, they fell asleep in each other's arms.

Early the next morning, Tony and Sugar were awakened by the sweet smell of hickory smoked bacon, coffee, and the pleasant sound of humming. When the permeating aroma seeped into Sugar's nostrils, she smiled and rose straight up in the bed out of her sleep.

"That's my Grandmamma!" she said out loud. Tony smiled and shook his head.

"Look at you," he said laughing. "You smelled that food and sat straight up outta your sleep."

"That's right! My Grandmamma in there throwing down for her baby," she said before delivering a quick kiss on his cheek and making a mad dash to the bathroom to wash up. Tony laughed and shook his head as he laid his back up against the headboard. Seeing Sugar this happy was like a little kid left all alone in a toy store. But she deserved every bit of it after having to endure a painful childhood without parents. Fortunately for her, God blessed her by filling that huge void with a sweet and loving grandmother who did a wonderful job raising her, and who thought the world of her and vice versa.

Not long after breakfast, Tony went outside to place a call to Genie to get briefed on the situation on the streets back home.

"Hey, Genie. What's up?"

"Oh it ain't nothing, bruh. Everythang, everythang. And I would like you to inform you that not only is Mr. Nathan Ward now a man without friends and an organization, and he's also run out of hiding places because we know the exact location where he's cowering at." Hearing this, Tony's face displayed a menacing grin.

"Okay Genie, and what about the other niggas?"

"Oh they're all taking cool and comfortable dirt naps right about now."

"That's what's up. But bruh, just remember my instructions. I don't want Mr. Ward touched."

"Yeah I know, T. And he's all yours whenever you ready for him, my brother. So how's the weather in the sunshine state?"

"Hot as hell! But we're really having a nice time though. In fact, Genie, we may even need to check out the market here." Genie laughed.

"Bruh, you supposed to be on vacation. So would you just get your mind off business for a change?"

"Now, Genie, you know that's an impossibility. Business is always on my mind front and center. Even when I'm sleep."

"I know, bruh, but try to enjoy yourself anyway."

"Will do."

"Alright bruh. Later man." After hanging up, Tony stood there with all kinds of homicidal thoughts surging through his brain concerning the news of Natty Boy. *I've got big plans for that muthafucka when I get back,* he thought to himself.

Later that evening, Sugar gave Tony an official tour of her neighborhood and the city. During the tour, she hinted a couple times about her desire to relocate back home one day and the hints didn't miss Tony either. Without Sugar's knowledge, he decided to secretly prospect for a home to surprise her with later. After the tour of her neighborhood ended, they went to Disney World for a few hours. This trip to Disney World for Tony was one that was long awaited. When he was a shorty his father promised him he would take him, but was never able to fulfill that promise because of his untimely death.

Much later that evening Sugar and Tony, accompanied by some of Sugar's old friends and relatives, went out to the club. While at the club, a couple of Sugar's old partners in crime who used to use her to set up drug dealers for a robbery showed up. One of them who had a thing for her was happy to see her, but not too thrilled to see her with a nigga.

"What's up, Sugar? Who this nigga you got with you?" he asked her, looking Tony up and down with contempt.

"This nigga here is my old man, nigga," she said with a half frown. "Tony, this is an old friend of mine, Dino. Dino this is Tony." Tony extended a handshake, but dude ignored him.

"Old friend? That's all I was? More like we was an item once upon a time," he said, grinning and looking over at Tony. Tony's green eyes turned to small slits.

"Once upon a time is right. Like ancient history, once upon a time," Sugar said, punching him in the chest. "Look, negro! Am I gone have to show my ass in this bitch, tonight?" she said with her hand in her purse. "Because you know me and this straight razor don't mind at all." Dude looked at her purse and then looked into Sugar's eyes. Seeing that they didn't blink once, he realized she meant business.

"Kee kee kee kee!" he laughed. "Girl, you know I'm just fucking with y'all. We cool, man," he said, extending his hand to Tony. "We good. I have no beef. I'm Dino."

"Cool. Good to meet you, Dino," Tony said, looking him in his eyes as he shook his hand so hard he could hear the bones cracking.

"Damn, nigga. I can see you have a strong grip, too," Dino said, shaking his hand. Sugar looked at Tony with that proud girlfriend look on her face.

"Where is the rest of the old crew, Dino?"

"Sugar, you know Q-Tip got murdered. Dre is doing time and Short is in here somewhere in the club."

"Nooooooo! Really? I didn't know that about Q-Tip. No one told me."

"Well, that's because you act like you don't know folks no more. Once you left it was like you forgot about us."

"No, that's not true, Dino. My life just headed in a whole nother direction. If I hadn't broke away from this place doing what I was doing, either I was going to end up dead like Q-Tip or in prison like Dre. Speaking of Q-Tip, what happened to him?" Dino took a sip of his drink before answering.

"What you think happened? He was still trying to lay folks down solo and got caught slipping. Make it so bad a bitch killed him."

"A female killed him?"

"Yep. He stepped down on this dope nigga from Miami in dude's crib and took his eyes off the nigga's girl who had a pistol in her bra. When he turned his back away from her she capped him right there in his neck. They took him and dumped him at the incinerator site where someone found what was left of him. He was still alive when the animals had started to eat on him. He later died at the hospital. The coroner assured his folks that when the scavengers started feasting on him he didn't suffer none since he was paralyzed from the neck down from the bullet."

"Okay. Okay. I don't wanna hear anymore," Sugar said with her hands over her ears. Her eyes had begun to well up with tears.

"Is his momma still here in Orlando? I'm going to go by and see her before I leave."

"No. After that happened to Q, she moved back to Jacksonville. I heard she had a stroke and is now in a nursing home, bed ridden. I guess after losing her last son she couldn't deal with it."

"Okay. That's enough of this bad news. Tony, let's go dance, baby," she said, grabbing him by the hand and dragging him to the dance floor. Sugar never told Tony that she used to set dope niggas up to get robbed by Dino and his crew.

After dancing to four straight songs, Tony and Sugar went and sat down at the big table with her friends and relatives. Before long, the club became packed with wall to wall niggas. It reminded Tony of a smaller version of the Calypso. The only difference with the crowd was the dress of the people, which was predominantly summer wear, which was understandable since they were in the Sunshine State where there was no need for the furs, bomber jackets, trench coats and heavy suits like in the bone chilling climate of New York. However, just like NY, there were cats in gangster attire and outside in the parking lot with the same gangster rides you would see there.

"Baby, I gotta go take a leak. Be back in a second," he said before kissing her on the cheek. The whole time, Dino never took his eyes off Tony and Sugar. The jealousy was seething from him as he downed drink after drink. It seemed like he was trying to drink himself into enough courage to pick back up where he left off when he first met Tony.

After Tony took a leak and went to the sink to wash his hands, the restroom door swung open and two cats walked in. Standing in front of the mirror, Tony noticed one of those cats was Dino.

"Hey nigga," Dino said, smiling. "Do you always have your bitches to fight your battles for you?"

Drying his hands off and looking up at Dino through the mirror he responded. "Excuse me. Are you talking to me?" Tony asked. Dino laughed.

"Who the hell else I'm talking too, nigga? You the only nigga I'm looking at, and the only one in this club who had his bitch to take up for him tonight." Tony laughed.

"Okay, Mr. Dino. Look! First of all, whatever thing you and Sugar had once upon a time, I could care less about that shit because that was before my time. Secondly, not now and not ever, is she anybody's bitch. Not mine. Not yours. She's a woman in every aspect of the word, you dig? Third, I didn't need her to stand in or stand up for me. She did that on her own, because that is the kinda shit a *real* woman does. They have their man's back, as I have hers, *always*. Now it seems that you and I got off to a bad start. How about we do this shit all over again?" Tony said, extending his hand. There was a flush in the stall where a dude was in taking a dump that broke the brief silence between Tony's handshake overtures. Dino's eyes rotated between Tony and his extended hand.

"Fuck nigga, I don't wanna be your friend. And I don't shake hands with people I don't like." Tony laughed and took his hand back.

"Okay," he said, smiling. "Can't say I didn't try, Mr. Dino. Now can you so kindly step aside, sir? You're kinda blocking my path, and crowding me here. Small spaces like bathrooms make me claustrophobic. Besides, I have to get back to my babygirl, Sugar. I'm sure she's missing me right about now," he said, with a provocative tone. At this time Tony could clearly see what was on Dino's mind. He was trying to decide whether or not it was worth it to take this beef to another level while monitoring Tony's eyes for any signs of softness in him. Seeing there was none, but instead a man who had something dangerous in his eyes, he concluded it was in his best interest to step aside.

"Okay, Mr. Tony," he said offering a fake smile. "I'm going to let you be on your way to your babygirl."

"Appreciate that, Mr. Dino." Just as Tony tried to walk past him, he finally built up enough nerve and swung on him with an overhand right that missed its mark as Tony ducked. Before Dino could recover, Tony shot him one to the jaw, followed by a kick to the chest that sent Dino crashing into the trash can in the corner. After Dino recovered and popped back to his feet, realizing that he didn't have hands for this dude standing in front of him in a martial arts stance, he attempted to reach into his waist, but before he could complete the task, Tony's right hand moved like a blur through the air. When the metal of the nickel plated .45 came into contact with the right side of Dino's face, it sounded like a shotgun going off. The blow sent Dino crumbling face first into the urinal. He was on his knees face down as if he was praying to the Porcelain God. Tony walked over to him and disarmed him of the .38 snub nose he attempted to pull from his waist. The cat who had been taking a shit in the far stall, finally emerged from it.

"*God damn!*" he said, looking at Dino as he made his way to the sink to wash his hands.

"Friend of yours?" Tony asked with his .45 still in his hand.

"Nah. Not at all. I don't fuck with niggas like this. He's a scum of the earth, po hustling jacker."

"Did you shoot the nigga?" he asked Tony. "It damn sure sounded like it."

"No. Bullets cost money," Tony said before placing his .45 back inside his holster inside his suit jacket. He then emptied the bullets from the Dino's snub nose into the toilet and threw the gun in the trash.

"Ummm hmmm," the cat said looking at Dino. "You done fucked around and got dealt with. You lucky this nigga was nice enough not to kill your ass. I would have," the O.G. said. Dino didn't hear none of that shit. He was still out cold, face down in the urinal. Tony looked in the mirror and straightened up his tie and was about to walk out when the O.G. extended his hand.

"Hey, my brother, I'm Big Roy," he said as Tony shook his hand.

"What's up? I'm Tony. Nice to meet you, Big Roy. Hey, I'm not trying to be funny, but I'm kinda claustrophobic and therefore don't like small, cramped places. I also don't make it a habit to chop it up with cats I just met in a bathroom. So let's continue this outside, if you don't mind, sir." Big Roy laughed.

"I understand, man. Besides, I did stink it up there. My damn stomach been tore up every since I got back from Miami." When they were walking out, a brother entered in and walked passed Dino as if he wasn't even there and started taking a piss in the urinal next to the one he was still face down in.

"Can I buy you a drink, Big Roy?" Tony asked.

"Why thank you, Tony, but no thanks. I gave that oil up ten years ago."

"Is that right?" Tony said smiling. "I gave it up the first time I got drunk and was thrown in the brig for it." They both laughed.

"The brig, you say?"

"Yep. The brig. A very cramped place."

"Sounds like someone been in the Corp."

"Yep. Ten years. Straight out of high school to Afghanistan."

"I knew it was something about you I liked other than knocking punks out. I was in the Corp myself. Did my time in 'Nam."

"Is that right?" Tony said. "Semper Fi, my brother."

"Semper Fi, Tony."

"Well, what is it you do here in the Sunshine State, Roy?"

"Ummmm a little of this and a little of that. You dig?" he said, smiling.

"Yeah, I dig." Tony smiled back.

"And you. What do you do, Tony, in...in? You never did say where you were from."

"New York. Brooklyn."

"Okay. What do you do in Brooklyn?"

"A little of this and a little of that." Roy laughed and took a sip of his Coke.

"Okay. I see. You here on vacation to get you some sun?"

"Something like that. I'm here with my woman who's visiting her grandmother."

"Oh okay. That someone wouldn't happen to be, Sugar is it?"

"Yeah. Just so happens that it is. You know Sugar?" Roy laughed.

"Not only do I know her, I'm her uncle."

"Well, I'll be damned. Small world, ain't it?" Tony said smiling.

"I heard she was in town, but I haven't had a chance to see her yet. I *just* got in from Miami a couple hours ago. That little situation in the bathroom was about Sugar, wasn't it?" Tony nodded his head.

"Yeah, I had to pistol whip that punk before about Sugar a few years ago. I never understood what she saw in him. But hey. Where is my niece at now?"

"She's probably at the table wondering what's taking her man so long to come back from the shitter."

"You mean she's in here right now?"

"Yeah. Over at that table over there. Follow me." Tony said smiling.

When Roy and Tony reached the table, Sugar was busy entertaining her friends and relatives.

"Hey girl," Roy said, tapping Sugar on her shoulders. "You still robbing folk's sugar containers?"

Immediately, Sugar knew who he was without even seeing his face.

"*Uncle Roy!*" she screamed as she jumped up in his arms.

"Careful now. Uncle Roy can't pick you up like he used too," he said laughing.

"Oh stop it. You are still the big strong Uncle Roy I've always known. How did you know I was in here? I called you and couldn't reach you to let you know I was coming home."

Clutching Tony's shoulder he said, "I was informed by this gentleman of your presence. Met him in the shitter." Laughter filled the table. By this time, the club's security was dragging Dino out of the club. Still almost out on his feet, he was still feeling the effects of that cold steel to the dome.

"Is that Dino?" Sugar asked.

"Yeah, that's his ass," a lady at her table said. "Somebody got with his ass. Always talking shit and grabbing his gun when somebody get ready to beat his ass." Tony and Roy smiled at each other without commenting. Sugar looked at them as if she suspected something was up.

"So Sugar Momma, how long you and Tony here for?"

"We're going to be here for a few more days. When are you coming to New York? All the time I've been there, you never visited other than when you helped me move there."

"Sugar Momma, now you know how I feel about that cold ass weather. All those years living in Chicago and Milwaukee forever turned me off from winter other than the one here in Florida. When me and that bitch gotta divorce, that was it for me. I moved back the *same day* the papers were signed." Sugar fell on him laughing.

"Uncle Roy, ain't nobody told you to marry that young girl," she said still laughing.

"Well, Uncle Roy need a young girl to keep his ticker, among a few other things, in working order. She just wasn't the one I needed. I don't know how many nights I came close to wasting that whore." The table again erupted in laughter.

"That's exactly why you should have sat your butt down somewhere and stayed with Aunt Mary."

"Listen here, Sugar Momma, let an old man school you on something. Women like Mary will always be there for men like me. She knew when she married me I was a whore. Now as far as my own self, the *only* thing I want that's old is my Cognac, my music, and my rides." Again, the table erupted in laughter.

"Now that's cold, Uncle Roy," she said laughing.

"Sugar Momma, this is a cold existence we live in," he said smiling. Tony pondered Roy's words and was reminded about the situation at home and the cold nature and dog eat dog of the streets. A place that was just as vicious and dangerous if not more than any jungle. A place where there were predators, scavengers, and prey, but something far worse than that, there were elements absent from a jungle called treachery and betrayal.

"Well hey, Sugar Momma, I've gotta go handle some business. As I said, I just got back in town. I'm going to come by ya grandmamma's house tomorrow to spend some time with y'all, okay? Maybe we can go to dinner or something."

"Okay, Uncle Roy. That would be nice. I am so glad to see you. I missed you and everyone else so much."

"And this is why you either need to move back home or visit more often, young lady," he said, placing a kiss on her forehead. "Tony, you take care of my favorite niece. It was a pleasure to meet you, my brother. We gonna have to sit down and rap a taste on a couple of things before y'all tear out."

"Likewise Roy. And no doubt, we will definitely talk." The two shook hands and Roy strolled out of the club followed by two of his men.

"Bye Uncle Roy," Sugar yelled to him.

The next day, Tony took Sugar to visit her brother, Horace, who was on the ass end of a ten year bid at Marion Correctional for manslaughter. When they arrived, they found out he was on lockdown and therefore lost his visitation privileges. Nearly ten years earlier, Horace killed a man over a car he had loaned him. The cat he killed, nicknamed Goliath, was a hulking figure of a man. A 6'11" 325 pound former NFL player turned neighborhood terror, who was banned from the league after serving an 8 year sentence for raping his young babysitter.

The story was, Horace, who was into collecting cars, let Goliath borrow his vintage '64 Chevy convertible. After several attempts to get his prized vert back from dude who had been talking shit that he had sold it and wasn't giving Horace shit back, Horace confronted him at the club. When Horace asked him to come outside and talk to him in the parking lot, dude walked outside and got in his face, pushed him and told him, "Nigga, what's this shit I been hearing in the street about you going around talking about stepping to me about that piece of shit car? Nigga, I sold the muthafucka. Now *what?*"

Horace hadn't mentioned to anyone that he was going to confront him. No one other than the people who Goliath had been bragging to knew about the situation with the car. In fact, a female of Goliath's urged him to return Horace's car and he slapped her and accused her of fucking him. The allegation was just Goliath's way of excusing the fucked up shit he had done to someone who did him a favor to help him out after being down on his luck. Without saying one word to Goliath and not so much as making a facial gesture that could be read, Horace took three steps back, pulled out a .357 magnum and shot Goliath in the right knee cap that crumbled him to the pavement. He laid there screaming and writhing in pain and holding his knee as he levied curses at Horace who just stood there peering down at him as if he was admiring his work.

The .357 bullet caused Goliath's knee cap to literally explode. Shards of bone and blood were all over the front of his pants leg and the ground as he laid there in a fetal position holding his knee in a puddle of blood. Horace sat on the hood of a car, and popped a piece of gum in his mouth, looking as if he was contemplating on whether he should finish the job or not amidst the pleas from bystanders begging him not to kill him. Someone in the crowd broke away and got his Uncle Roy who was next door hanging out at Charlie Town Bar where the triple O.G. cats post up at. When Roy arrived, Horace was still there calmly sitting on the hood of a car with his gun laid across his lap, chewing gum and looking down at Goliath who was holding his knee and continuously cursing. Roy urged Horace not to kill him as were many others standing around. When it appeared that Horace was going to walk off and spare Goliath's life, he levied a threat that made Horace stop dead in his tracks.

After momentarily pondering the threat on his life, and amidst the various voices urging him not to kill him, Horace turned around, quickly walked up to him and unloaded the revolver into him. His 325 pound frame lifted off the ground with each shot. Fortunately, Horace's lack of a record and his Uncle Roy's association with some very important people downtown, not to mention the high powered lawyer he retained for him, he only received ten years. Word was, just before turning himself in, Horace found out who Goliath sold his ride to and paid him a visit. By the time Horace left, he got his car back without incident, all except for a not so idle threat against the gentleman's life.

Sugar had never mentioned her brother to Tony. In fact, Sugar never even mentioned that she had a brother. Tony would later find out that Horace was a cold blooded killer who was never caught for several other killings he had committed, which is why it was so easy to kill Goliath. Sugar explained that she had heard rumors in the family that Horace was a hitter, though he never let her know that. Looking at him no one would ever know what he did for a living. He looked like a nerdy school boy version of Terrence Howard with glasses. That innocent off brand look of his would cause at least two hard core convicts at Marion to underestimate him and get shanked for their troubles. One had to be life flighted out to an outside hospital.

Over the next couple of weeks, Tony and Sugar spent a great deal of time with her grandmother and other relatives, having a ball in O-Town. In fact, more fun than Tony had in a long time, probably since he was a youngster back in Atlanta. However, as the old saying goes, all good things must come to an end, and the day finally came when it was time for Tony and Sugar to go home. This scene was even more emotional than the first, with the two women, granddaughter and grandmother hugging each other tightly as they both cried their eyes out. Taken aback, Tony stood there somewhat helpless and lost for words at one point. In a quick witted attempt to bring some form of comfort to the emotional situation, he intervened.

"Hey, babygirl! Did you mention to your Grandma about us looking for a house here?" All teary eyed, Sugar turned to face him with a bewildered look on her face.

"Uh no, I forgot to tell her," she said with her eyes silently questioning him.

With her own tears streaming down her cheeks, Grandma looked at Sugar and said, "Are y'all really looking for a house here, baby, or is y'all just tryin' to make Grandma feel better about y'all leaving?" Not wanting to lie to her, Sugar hesitated in answering her question as she looked over at Tony.

"Oh yes, ma'am!" he said, bailing Sugar out. "We are seriously looking for a place here in Orlando. In fact, I think it would be a wonderful place to live and perhaps raise children."

"Oh baby!" Grandma said as she reached up to hug him. "You really are a God send to my baby!"

"No Grandmamma, you are the real God send," he said, embracing her tiny frame, and looking over at Sugar, who still had the bewildered look on her face.

A few minutes later and saying the last goodbye, Tony packed the last pieces of luggage, bags of new clothes and souvenirs they brought from the shopping malls into the rental car, and he and Sugar set off to the airport.

Within a few hours, and shortly after the plane touched down back in the concrete jungle, Tony and Sugar arrived at their new crib. As soon as they finished unpacking, Tony immediately got right down to the business of Natty Boy Ward with no further delay, by placing a call to Genie and setting up a meeting, with him, the Professor, and Macky Boy. Before leaving, he kissed Sugar on the forehead.

"Babygirl, I've got some very urgent business to take care of, so I'll see you a little later on tonight."

"Okay, baby, but before you go, I wanna thank you again for saying that to make my Grandmamma feel better about us leaving," Sugar said as Tony stood at the door putting on a trench coat and matching hat.

"You're welcome, babygirl. But I wasn't just saying it to make your granny feel good. I was serious." Suddenly, Sugar leaped from the sofa and ran up to him and placed kisses all over his face.

"That's exactly why I love you, baby!" she said.

"So is this the only reason you love me?" he smiled and asked.

"Along with a thousand and one other reasons, Mr. Stall-worth." she said giving him one last passionate kiss before he left to go meet with his men.

As soon as Tony arrived in his upstairs office at the Calypso, he sat down at his desk, and immediately got down to the business at hand.

"Alright. Where is Mr. Ward hiding?" Genie nodded to Macky Boy for him to elaborate.

"We tracked him to his hometown in Atlanta, after being tipped off by one of his soldiers during an interrogation. He's hiding in one of his penthouses off Highway 85 that leads to town. He has some of his relatives and friends acting as his security now that he's all out of soldiers." Tony stared straight ahead in silence, and not once breaking his gaze.

"Well, go get the nigga!" he said.

Chapter 23

Natty Boy's Last Ride

Later that night, Tony got a knock at his front door, and when he opened it, Genie was standing there taking sips from a silver flask, with a sinister grin on his face.

"'Sup bruh? That package has arrived."

"Where?" Tony asked. Genie motioned his head to the car parked in his driveway where Macky Boy and two of his soldiers stood at the trunk. Tony walked over to the trunk and Macky Boy popped it open, revealing a sweaty, butt naked, bound and gagged Natty Boy. His fright filled eyes were stretched as big as saucers and spoke volumes about his dilemma. Tony momentarily stared down at him with no expression on his face.

"Mr. Nathan Ward, glad to have you with us," he said as he slammed the trunk down just as Natty Boy muffled a few words in an attempt to plead his case. Genie chuckled then took another sip from his flask.

"Okay, T, what you want done with the nigga?"

"Meet me at the zoo in half an hour." Genie, Macky Boy and the two soldiers hopped in the '64 Lincoln with the suicide doors and sped off with Natty Boy's ass bumping around in the trunk.

A half hour later at Prospect Park Zoo, one of Tony's soldiers popped opened the trunk and instantly, the smell of musk, shit, and urine completely filled the air causing the animals to immediately react. The stench and fear that Natty Boy exuded through his pores sent them into a frenzy, because their instincts alerted them to the presence of death. As Tony, Genie, and Macky Boy stood there a few feet from the car, the two muscle bound soldiers reached inside the trunk and pulled Natty Boy out by his neck before leading him to the ledge of the Polar Bear exhibit. His legs shook so badly, he could barely stand up. His mind told him to break and run, but his legs refused to cooperate. So he just stood there trembling, butt naked, and looking around all wide-eyed. *Why did we have to fuck with this nigga here?* Natty Boy thought to himself. Facing his own mortality, a plethora of emotions surged through his brain while four stern faces stared at him. *He gave us a good deal we should have been happy with, and I tried to convince them niggas of this, but they wasn't trying to hear that. Now I'm the only one left here at the zoo all alone and it ain't looking good.*

Tony reached and snatched off the tape from Natty Boy's mouth, removing both skin and mustache along with it. The high-pitched screams of the monkeys and deafening roars of the lions and other big cats increased a few decibels as they seemed to sense the inevitable. The animals' savage outbursts were absolutely chilling, and only seemed to compound Natty Boy's fears. He jerked his head from side to side to look around as though he was anticipating one of the screaming beasts to pounce on him at any moment.

"Look Tony! I-I-I had nothing to do with-with-with it, man!" he said stuttering and looking down behind him. His heels were just inches away from the edge of the Polar Bear pit. Awakened by all the commotion, some of the bears had begun to file out of their dens to investigate. After seeing the men standing at the top of the ledge, and perhaps thinking it was dinner time, they all wandered up to the edge and looked up at the butt naked human with keen curiosity. When Natty Boy looked down to see this gathering of bears directly a few feet below where he stood, this precipitated a more intense round of begging.

"Tony! Tony! Look man! Let me explain man!"

"Okay. I'm listening. But let me save you some trouble and keep it gutter with you. You ain't talking your way outta this shit. I'm sure you know when we brought you here to this zoo in the trunk butt naked, bound, and gagged, we were past conversation.

In fact, you had to have known that you and I were at the proverbial point of no return. And tonight represents the last sentence in the final chapter in our story. But be my guest. Say what's on your mind. I'm all ears." Tony replied calmly, looking him straight in his eyes with a blank stare.

"Please believe me, man! It was Cat Eye Jones and…and… the others! They are the ones who tried to off you. I agreed to the deal, but they overruled me on it." Tony just stood there stone-faced not saying a word, his face said it all. *Go ahead and explain nigga, but you ain't talking your way out of this shit!*

"I swear, Tony! I swear to God, man! I had nothing to do with it!" Genie took a long sip from his flask and let out a wicked laugh that echoed throughout the entire zoo.

"Stop lying, nigga! And stop your goddamn begging! God ain't gotta damn thing to do with this either! " he said with utter contempt. "You know goddamn well you and those fuck niggas tried to murk my man, even after he tried to share the wealth with you crab ass niggas, so everybody could eat! But how did you show your gratitude? Y'all muthafuckas tried to have him and his woman hit!"

Genie's words seem to re-evoke Tony's anger as Natty Boy continued to beg and plead his case without pause. Without saying another word, Tony planted a vicious kick square to Natty Boy's chest causing him to flip over into the polar bear pit flat on his back. Before he could hit the ground good, the bears were all over his ass. His blood curdling screams totally drowned out the animal noises in the zoo. The polar bears, from the young to the old, had him encircled and feasting on him alive, ripping out his intestines and tearing off his limbs. The zoo animals went absolutely berserk over the smell of blood as Tony and his men stood stone-faced at the edge of the pit looking down at the gruesome spectacle, until Natty Boy's screams finally subsided to faint gurgles. After a few more moments of the carnivores making short

CATO

work of him, each of them tearing off their share of the fresh meat before running away to dine in private, and no more signs of life, Tony and his men walked stoically away from the scene, hopped into their rides and drove away.

Making his early rounds the following morning, which included feeding the animals, Norman Byrd who had been the zookeeper for the past twenty years, after relocating to Brooklyn from Mississippi, was surprised to see that the bears had already been fed after noticing one of the cubs gnawing on a piece of meat.

"Damn! I wonder who the hell fed the bears when I'm the head nigga in charge of feeding," he said proudly. "Musta been one of them lil' bad as kids from Harlem that was here yesterday on the school field trip. I hate them lil' bastards anyway and I done told them lil' muthafuckas not to be feedin' my damn animals. Let me catch another one doing it. Imma put them, their mammies and their pappies outta here!" he said, mumbling as he continued to walk up to the pit. "Whatever that is you gnawing on lil' buddy, it shole looks kinda funny," he said to one of the cubs. "Don't look like nothing I ever fed you."

Unable to make out what the cub was feeding on, he took out his binoculars to conduct a closer examination of the pit. "Damn it, man! Where did all this damn blood come from?" he said aloud. As he investigated a little further, he noticed what appeared to be a gutted out animal carcass near the entrance to the den. "I know goddamn well that ain't no whole animal carcass, because we don't have that on the menu here." As he walked slowly around the exhibit, closely scanning and inspecting the yard, something caught his attention. That something was a partially eaten human skull. The zookeeper screamed to the top of his lungs in horror.

The violent end to the iconic and flamboyant Natty Boy Ward, Cat Eye Jones and their syndicate partners who ruled the five boroughs for over four decades with impunity, not only in-jected fear in the collective hearts of everyone whoever even thought about crossing Tony Stallworth, it also helped tighten his grip on the coke trade in the tri-states, and further etched his rep-utation in stone. His distribution network now extended into the west coast and penetrated parts of Florida, moving over 1,500 kilos a month and raking in tens of millions of dollars with near complete impunity from law enforcement and competitors alike. After this incident, the word reverberated throughout every cor-ner and dope trap in the city and beyond - You either roll with Tony Stallworth and benefit, or you get rolled over.

CATO

Chapter 24

Traitor in the Ranks

Later that year after Tony and Sugar exchanged wedding vows in a private ceremony, they went on their honeymoon in the Cayman Islands where they enjoyed a week and a half of much needed time away from the hustle and bustle of the city life. However, unbeknownst to them, it would be the last time they would have fun for some time to come, due to the trouble taking shape at home. As Tony's power and influence had increased, so did the animosity and resentment. The ancient identical twins of jealousy and envy had begun to rear their ugly heads once again, but this time within the ranks of Tony's own organization. This would inevitably set off a chain of events that would soon transform his and Sugar's world forever.

Shortly after arriving at JFK airport, Tony and Sugar grabbed their luggage and were about to walk out of the lobby when ten men brandishing badges and pointing guns, surrounding them.

"Alright, Mr. Antonio Stallworth, don't move! You're under arrest!" the lead officer, a tall Frankenstein looking cat said.

"*Under arrest? Under arrest for what?*" Tony said, dropping his bags before two cops grabbed his arms and handcuffed him.

"For the murder of Nathan Ward, Mr. Stallworth, and I'm sure you know *exactly* what I'm talking about, so don't play dumb with me," Frankenstein said before letting out a wicked laugh.

"*Murder! What the fuck are y'all crackers talking about?*" Sugar asked, angrily.

"Ma'am, if you don't wanna go with your old man, you better step back. Your husband is taking a little trip downtown with us, so don't wait up for him, because he may be taking the long ride this time," Frankenstein said, while the other officers frisked Tony.

"Babygirl, do as they say. I'll be alright. Just be cool and go to the house."

"Alright, Mr. Stallworth, you have the right to remain silent."

"Yeah, yeah man, I know all that shit! So you can just save your breath, and get me on to the station so I can contact my lawyer." After watching her man being quickly ushered away, Sugar placed a call to Genie.

"Hello, Genie here."

"Genie, they got Tony! They got Tony!"

"Who, Sugar? Who got Tony?" Genie said frantically.

"The crackers!" she replied. "They arrested him at the airport for murder!"

"Okay, Sugar. I'mma need for you to calm down, baby. I'll call and find out what's going on, okay? Just be cool. We have our own personal bondsman, so if he gets a bond, we will spring him right away, okay?"

"Okay, Genie, but please make sure you call me the minute you hear something!"

"Aight, Sugar. I'll do just that, but in the meantime I want you to be cool and don't worry, okay? I'll take care of everything." After hanging up, Sugar sat there on the couch stressing over Tony, but quickly regained her composure after remembering what he often said to her. *In the face of crisis and adversity, a cool head is your greatest asset.* Tony had certainly schooled her well, and little did he know, it was about to pay off in a big way.

A couple hours later, Genie dropped by to update Sugar on Tony's situation.

"'Sup, Sugar," he said as he walked through the door.

"Well?" she asked.

"Sit down for a second, Sugar." She sat down on the couch beside him, and stared at him waiting on an answer.

"Tony is being held without bond right now."

"Without bond?"

"Yeah, baby, without bond. But that's at least for now. They have him charged with an open count of murder." Sugar looked down at the floor.

"But Sugar, that's not all. It gets worse."

"What is it, Genie?"

"They have a warrant for me as well on the same charge."

"What!"

"Yep," he said, nodding his head. Sugar sat there speechless and lost for words. "Yeah, I seriously believe some muthafucka in the organization ratted us out! In fact, I would put everything on it."

"Real talk, Genie? You have any idea who it could be?"

"Yeah, I have my list of suspects, but hell all those nigga are suspects as far as I'm concerned. Eventually, we will know exactly who. But in the meantime, I'm going to turn myself in tomorrow morning, but before I do, I have some important instructions for you from Tony."

"Instructions? What instructions, Genie?" she asked with a bewildered look on face. Genie handed her an envelope.

"This here is the instructions Tony told me to give you in the event something happened to him."

Sugar looked at the envelope for a moment and smiled. "That's Tony for you. Always looking ahead," she said before her smile quickly transformed into a look of sadness. Genie held her hand.

"Everything gonna be alright, Sugar," he said, smiling. "This shit will be over with before you know it."

"Sure it will, Genie," she said, holding her head up high.

"That's my girl," he said, patting her hand. "Well okay Sugar, I'm going to take off now to take care of some loose ends before I turn myself in tomorrow."

"Well Genie, how is Selina taking all this?"

"Shiiiiiid!" he said, as he rose to his feet. "That broad disappeared immediately after that incident, and I ain't seen her ass since! Ole punk!" Sugar nearly fell off the couch laughing.

"Genie, you a fool!" she said with tears welling up in her eyes. "You can't blame her for not sticking around after that drama!"

"Yeah, I guess you right. But you stuck around with my man, T."

"Yeah, Genie, but I'm cut from a different cloth. I'm willing to kill or be killed for my man, because when I vowed death do us part, I meant that."

"Damn!" he said smiling. "I wish the good Lord would bless me with a woman with that same policy. I can't keep a woman!"

"You ain't gonna do right even if he did bless you with one," she said laughing.

"Yeah well, you may just have a point there, Sugar." They both laughed. Before leaving Genie turned to her and said, "I want you to know, Sugar, you are the best thing that ever happened to my dude. And I know this for a fact! We've been knowing one another since we were kids, and he's never had anyone quite like you in his life." Sugar smiled. "Now Sugar, you take heed to those instructions, because it just may save everything that Tony worked hard for, but more importantly, it may in fact save his life as well as yours." Sugar nodded slowly, as his words sunk in.

"Okay Genie, and thanks."

"Oh yeah, I ordered some extra security to post up outside and keep an eye on you until this shit is over." With that said, Genie walked out, leaving Sugar standing at the door to sort out her thoughts. Her eyes immediately shifted to the envelope in her hand. *I wonder what the instructions are in this envelope?* she thought to herself as she continued to stare at it. *Whatever it is, it must be important enough for Genie to come all the way over here and hand it to me personally, knowing he had a warrant out for him.*

Sugar walked over to the bar to fix herself a drink. After fixing her Hen and Coke, she sat down on the couch with the manila envelope still in her hand. After taking a sip she ripped it open and began scanning its contents. Besides the typical tasks for a wife to perform in her husband's absence, there was nothing in the letter earth shaking - that was until she got to the part that read, "In the event I am no longer capable of executing my business affairs, all power and authority will shift to Genie. However, if Genie is absent or unable to assume this responsibility, Sugar is next in line to assume this position and thus execute *any* and *all* business affairs. Absolute power and authority is hers."

Almost immediately, Sugar's adrenaline began flowing. She nervously downed her drink and headed back to the bar to fix another one, but this time without the chaser. *Okay chick, get it together,* she said to herself before downing the drink. The significance of the moment bore down on Sugar like a ton of bricks. To say the least, this was a heavyweight responsibility. A responsibility she never even imagined she would have to assume, not even in her wildest dreams, especially for someone who knew absolutely nothing about the business. Sure, she had been involved in some gangster shit in the past with her jacker homeboys, but nothing like this. The only responsibility she had in that was to look pretty and lure tender-dick, lust-struck niggas to a secluded area or a hotel room to get laid down and that shit was easy. But this shit here? This was an entirely different arena. But nevertheless, she knew what she had to do, and what needed to be done to save her man's organization, and perhaps his life. By

191

an unfortunate twist of fate, it was Sugar's time to reign now whether she wanted to or not, and reign she would.

The next morning, Sugar went to visit Tony on Riker's Island. As soon as she walked into the visitation booth and saw Tony, both of their eyes lit up. He blew her a kiss.

"What's up, babygirl! How are you holding up?" Tony said, through the glass.

"I'm good, Tony, baby. I'm just worried about you." Although she was pretending to be alright, Tony could see that she wasn't.

"Are you sure you're alright, baby?" he asked, monitoring her body language.

"Yeah, Tony. Really, I'm good."

"That's my Queen!" he said, smiling.

"Well, Tony, baby, what's going on with this situation? Genie told me he was being charged too."

"Yeah they're trying to pin Nathan Ward's murder on us."

"Are you talking about the man they found half eaten at the Prospect Zoo?" Tony nodded his head.

"Do they have anything?"

"No, babygirl, just someone implicating us, which don't amount to shit at the end of the day. They'll need a little more than a statement from some snitch."

"You have any idea who it is, Tony?"

"Yeah, babygirl. I have a hunch, but I'll fill you in later. As of right now, I don't think any of my men, including the Professor, know Genie and me been charged with Natty Boy's murder. For some reason it hasn't hit the news yet. So make sure you don't mention any details of it to any of them right now, at least not until the meeting, okay baby?"

"Okay."

"So, I take it you got my instructions?"

"Yeah, I got your instructions alright. Boy did I get them," she said as she exhaled. Tony laughed.

"So are you up to the task, babygirl?"

"Hell, I don't have any choice but to be up to the task."

"Yeah I know, babygirl. But sometimes in life you have to play the cards you're dealt. This is why I schooled you on a few things and never completely shut you out of what I do, and for situations like this. There are only two people on this planet I trust with my life. That's Genie and you, baby."

"I know," she said smiling and touching the visitation window that separated she and her man. "That's exactly why I won't let you down, baby."

"That's my Queen!" he said, smiling. "Okay, now babygirl, let me fill you in on a few very important things you need to remember. So listen to me carefully. If anybody, I mean *anybody,* in my organization step to you and mention anything about me and Genie being charged with Natty Boy's murder, or so much as ask anything concerning my situation, that person is the traitor in our ranks. Also, I want you to be extra careful and vigilant and pay close attention to your surroundings and everything at all times. Take nothing for granted, and don't underestimate nothing or no one, you dig?" Sugar nodded her head. "The reason I'm telling you all this is because I strongly suspect someone will try to make a move on my organization with me and Genie conveniently out of the way. So trust no one, not even the Professor. The only person in my organization I think will remain loyal to me is the youngster, Macky Boy. I admired him from the first time I met him, but even with him, be careful. Then there are ways of testing his loyalty to us, you feel me? Make sure also, that you keep the soldiers with you at all times, no matter what you're doing or where you go, keep them with you, okay?"

"Okay bae," she said with a slight feeling of apprehension.

"Oh, and don't give anyone a heads up about where you're going or what time you'll be there. I don't care if it's a meeting, a hair appointment, nail appointment, or lunch date with one of your friends."

"Don't worry, Tony. I got it."

"Oh yeah, babygirl, do you remember that lawyer cat Goldman who we met at the Japanese restaurant?" Sugar smiled.

"Of course I do. That was the night I put on that Oscar winning performance." Tony laughed. "Yeah, babygirl, that place. Give him a call and let him know I can use his services now."

"Okay. I'll take care of it. Well, baby, is Genie here yet? He said he was going to turn himself in this morning."

"Yeah he's here. A guard told me he was still in central booking, but I pulled some strings to get him in the same unit with me. Well okay, babygirl, the guard just motioned for me to wrap it up, but you take care and remember everything I told you here today, okay?"

"Okay baby. I will. But baby before you go, there is one condition I have for me to hold this thing down for you."

"Ooookay," he said with a half-smile. "And what condition is that, babygirl?"

"The condition that I have is that all this ends whenever this situation is resolved. I'm not saying that it should end immediately, because even I know that you can't just shut things down abruptly and close up shop. But I'm talking about a transition that will close this chapter and begin a new one without all the drama that comes with this life. And I know you know something about closing chapters because you've done it before with no regrets and no hesitation. The type of bread you have accumulated, with your mind and organizational skills, along with my accountant skills, we can do anything we wanna do, baby, in terms of business. I have some extremely good business ideas for us that I promise will stimulate you just as much as the fast money. I don't know how it is to be a black man and I won't dare to pretend as if I do, but I do know that black men have to rise above not only the bullshit that they have to deal with on a daily basis, but their own mindsets and short sightedness that hold them back. This includes being out on the corner or caught up in the gangster shit to make money in dead end, and unfulfilling hustles." Tony smiled and nodded in approval.

"Yes, babygirl, I do know sumpin' about closing chapters and consider this one closed when I'm on the other side with you. You not only have a deal, you have my word. I love you, baby-girl," he said as he placed a kiss on the window before being led away by the guard. Sugar sat there for a moment so she could regain her composure before exiting the visitation booth. It was heartbreaking to see her man in such a helpless situation, but she knew this wasn't the time to be emotional because with the monumental task facing her, there was no room for that weak human attribute. In fact, she was going to have to be one strong, ruthless bitch to save her old man and his empire, perhaps more ruthless than him.

CATO

Chapter 25

Make Way for the Queen

Early the next morning around nine, Sugar met with attorney Goldman and gave him one hundred and fifty racks in cash to retain him for Tony and Genie. When Sugar opened the briefcase that contained the bread, Goldman's eyes nearly popped out of his eye sockets. To top it all off, before walking out, Sugar told him to take whatever he needed for his fees and keep the change. The next thing she did was call Armando to let him know that the show must and will go on, and he agreed. Afterwards, she called an emergency meeting of Tony's organization and within two hours they met at the usual meeting place in the conference room in the rear of Tony's grocery store in Queens. After all the members filed in and took their places at the round table, Sugar took her place at the podium with the Professor standing at her side.

"Alright, gentlemen," the Professor said, "we called this meeting here today because Mrs. Stallworth has an important announcement to make, so listen up."

"Thank you, Professor," she said before turning to face the men. "Okay. Some of y'all know me as Mrs. Stallworth, but you can call me Sugar. I'm here today to announce a temporary successor in Tony's absence just as he instructed me to do." Hearing this, the Professor stood there with a confident look on his face that he would be the chosen one. Sugar continued. "Well, gentlemen, you're looking at the successor. Me!"

Almost instantly, the expression changed on the Professor's face from a look of confidence and exhortation to a mask of disappointment and resentment, but he knew he better not make it obvious. The members all started to make subtle body movement and facial gestures, but remained silent. Macky Boy, who never vibed with the Professor from the beginning, peeped out the hate on his face and cracked a smile. Seeing him not named the successor was a source of great amusement for him.

"Okay, now that we got that out of the way, everything is to remain like it was when Tony was here. The only difference being, I'm in charge now. So are there any questions, gentlemen?" she asked, but no one answered. "Well okay, this meeting is adjourned." Everyone filed out except the Professor and Macky Boy who stopped by on his way out and whispered in Sugar's ear. "

I don't know what's going on, ma'am, but if you need me for anything, I'm here, and I got your back." Sugar nodded. On the way out, Macky Boy cracked a grin at the Professor.

"I'm with you too, Sugar," he said walking up to her. "I'm with you one hundred percent."

"I'm glad to hear that Professor, because I'm gonna need all the backing I can get." Before turning and exiting the conference room the Professor asked, "Oh, by the way, did the crackers charge Genie with Natty Boy's murder also?"

Almost instantly, a huge lump developed in Sugar's throat and her heart started to race. A plethora of emotions went through her as Tony's words echoed in her brain as if he was standing their repeating them. *If anybody in my organization mentions anything concerning my situation, that person is the traitor in our ranks.* But she kept her composure and didn't let him notice her reaction.

"Yeah, Professor, they were both arrested on the same charge."

"Damn!" he said, shaking his head. "They will be alright, I'm sure."

"Oh, for sho'. They'll be just fine. I'm going to make sure of that myself, Professor."

Chapter 26

The Professor is the Traitor

The second visit to see her man at Riker's was easier than the first, but nonetheless stressful. The news she had for him didn't make matters any better, however. But the silver lining in it was now at least they knew who the nigga was who crossed Tony and Genie up.

"Hey, babygirl," Tony said before placing a kiss on the glass and sitting down inside the visitation booth.

"Hey, Tony, baby," she said, touching the glass.

"Hey, lil' mama. How you holding up?"

"I'm good, baby. How you are holding up is more important."

"Oh, besides a lack of comfort and not being able to sleep next to you, I'm good. But now that I see your lovely face, my day just got better," he said, smiling.

"Well hopefully you will have all that again, like real soon."

"No doubt, babygirl. Oh yeah, Genie finally made it in late last night. It took forever for him to go through booking, but he's good now."

"Oh great. Tell him I said hello."

"Okay, will do."

"Well, Tony, baby, I want you to compose yourself, because I have good news and bad news. So I will give you the good news first."

"Okay, let's have it," he looked into her eyes.

"The good news is, I believe I know who the traitor is. Now for the bad news. It's the Professor," she said as she monitored Tony's reaction. "He was the one who ratted on you."

Tony smiled and nodded his head without saying a word, which left Sugar somewhat confused.

"So you're not surprised, Tony?"

"No, babygirl, I'm not surprised at all. In fact, I figured it all along, I just needed some confirmation. It makes perfect sense. With me and Genie out of the equation, the Professor would be a lock for the top spot, or at least that's what he surmised. I had also heard from an unconfirmed source that he had been making inquiries in locating another plug."

"Damn, baby! You knew this all along and you didn't get rid of his ass?"

"No, babygirl. I didn't and have to admit I slipped on that one. I was so preoccupied with that recent situation we just brought closure to. I procrastinated on looking a little deeper into it."

"Well, no sense in worrying about it now. What's done is done. And it is what it is. Now we just have to handle it. I got this."

"I know you do, babygirl. But check this out. The Professor wouldn't have dared make such an ambitious move like this if he didn't have allies within the organization. And something else, babygirl. Sooner or later he's going to try and assassinate you and me both, but I'm willing to bet he'll come after me first because with me out of the way, he can take the shipments and won't have to worry about any reprisals. He can convince the others to defy you with me out of the way. Damn!" he said, looking away with the phone in his hand. "I really fucked up big time on this one! I have always prided myself on not fuckin' up, and now I do it at a critical time like this."

"Okay, now look, Tony!" Sugar said in a stern voice and touched the screen. "Now is not the time to be having a pity party over some shit that we can't change now! We have to focus on the here and now, and what we gone do to fix this shit, you dig? The man I know and love don't cry over spilt milk, rather he cleans it up and just pours another glass!"

"That's my Queen," he said smiling. "I can see that the one thing I did succeed on is teaching you well."

"No doubt!" she said smiling.

"So, babygirl, were you able to read any of the other members at the meeting?"

"No, not really, but the youngster, Macky Boy, did approach me and assured he had my back."

"Yeah, that sounds like him," Tony said, smiling with a look of admiration on his face. "I was quite impressed with him the moment I met him. I believe he's very trustworthy, but test him anyway and see, babygirl. But remember, don't take nothing or no one for granted."

"Okay. I got it. But I can't wait for all this shit to be over so you can come home."

"Yeah, babygirl, who you telling? I'm ready to touch down *today*. But we have to play this shit out right. Right now they don't have anything other than a statement, so we just have to continue to play the game. It's all about a game and career advancement to the pigs, and if they can land a big fish like me, they can write their ticket. But I will play their game and at the end of the day when all the dust clears, I still be standing."

"You mean *we* will still be standing *together*, because I'm all in it with you to the end."

"True!" Tony said, smiling. Moments later the hack motioned to Tony that his time was up.

"Well, babygirl, it's that time again. But always remember everything I tell you and be safe. I love you," he said placing a kiss on the window.

"I love you, too, Tony," she said as the guard led him to the back.

CATO

Chapter 27

A Test of Loyalty

Later that night, Sugar sat at the crib looking over some figures from their grocery stores and other businesses, both legal and not so legal. Tony's legal businesses grossed less than three million while his illicit trade generated over two hundred million dollars annually, with the vast majority of that money going into overseas bank accounts, and two percent of his earnings going into inner city ventures like gated housing in the hood, recreational centers, shelters, business incubators, and other urban revitalization projects. Sugar's impeccable accounting skills at washing his money and reinvesting it into legit enterprises, made it all possible.

After finishing her work, she sat there for a few moments to gather her thoughts, before deciding it was time to plot and strategize. She recalled what Tony said that there were ways she could test the youngster. And she was going to do just that. It was time to put the youngster, Macky Boy, who was perhaps her sole ally in the organization, loyalty to Tony to the test.

After hopping out of the shower, Sugar oiled herself down with baby oil and slipped on a sexy negligee before placing a call to the young lieutenant to come through. Afterwards, she went into her bedroom and pulled a nickel plated .38 snub nose from her dresser and slipped it into the waistband of her panties in the small of her back before going to the bar in the living room to fix herself a glass of Hen and Coke. She then turned on some jazz, dimmed the lights and waited for the youngster to show up. About thirty minutes later, Macky Boy arrived. When Sugar opened the door, the youngster's eyes nearly exploded when he looked down to see what she was wearing.

"Come on in and have a seat, honey," she said with a flirta-tious smile. The youngster walked in all timid and sat down on the chair that was closest to the door.

"Would you like a drink or something, Macky Boy?" she asked as she walked back to the bar twisting her ass like a model on the runway. After clearing the lump in his throat he answered.

"No thank you, ma'am. I don't drink."

"Wait justa minute!" she said with her hands on her hips. "What is all this ma'am shit? Just call me Sugar, honey." Sweat had now begun to drip off the youngster's face as if he was rain-ing from the top of his head. Noticing his nervousness, Sugar moved closer to him and began to wipe the sweat from his face. "You okay, baby?" she asked. "Is it too hot in here or something? If it is, you can get more comfortable if you like."

"No...no, ma'am," he said. "I mean, no Mrs. Stallworth. I'm...I'm...I'm...I'm good," he stuttered.

"Well, you certainly don't look like you good, honey," she said before standing up and positioning her cat so close to his face he could probably smell the fragrance she used to sweeten it up with.

"Are you sure you, okay?" she asked. "Because if not, maybe some of this pussy will make you feel better." Finally, after tak-ing all he could take, Macky Boy suddenly sprung to his feet, gently pushing her aside.

"No ma'am!" he said. "I mean, no Mrs. Stallworth! You're Mr. Tony's woman!"

"Well, what's wrong? I'm not fine enough for you?" she asked as she cornered him.

"Yes! You look damn good! But I just can't do that to my boss!" Sugar smiled and nodded her head.

"Okay, Macky Boy. Have a seat, man," she said as the height-ened alert button in her mind was turned off. "You can relax now."

After he sat down slowly with a confused look on his face, she reached in the small of her back and pulled out the snub nose then placed it on the coffee table.

"I was just testing you," she said, smiling and taking a sip of her drink. "And you passed with flying colors, because not many men would have turned down this pussy." Macky Boy still wore the confused look on his face. Taking another sip of her Hen, she said, "Now you do know if you had flunked the test I was going to blow your muthafuckin' brains out, right?" He acknowledged by nodding his head in agreement.

"Tony likes you a lot, you know. He said you were stand up was his exact words," she said, walking over to the bar to fix her another drink.

"Yeah, that's how I'm cut. When I'm with you, I'm with you. Where I come from, my code is death before dishonor." Sugar sipped her Hen and monitored him carefully.

"I'm glad to hear that. I don't think that's the same policy for other members in Tony's organization."

"Who do you mean? The Professor?" he asked. Sugar stared at him for a second before responding.

"Yes. Especially, the Professor. So how did you know I meant him?"

"Because from the beginning I never liked or trusted that nigga. This morning at the meeting when you didn't name him as a successor, you could clearly see the hate on his face. Like I said, I never liked or trusted him."

"And you were right not to trust him, because he's the one who ratted Tony and Genie out to those crackers concerning Natty Boy's murder."

"*What!* Mrs. Stallworth, just give me the order and I will go murk that muthafucka *right now!*"

"Nah. Not just yet," she said, shaking her head. "There are others who are down with him, but we don't know who they are as of yet, which means we have to sit and lie in wait for the other traitors to show themselves."

"Do you have any idea who they may be?"

"No. Not at this time. But that's where you come in."

"Okay. But again, whatever you need me to do, just give me the orders." Sugar nodded her head.

"Okay, well, for right now this is what I want you to do. Go to the Professor and start talking negative about me being in charge and stress to him how he should be running things in Tony's absence instead of me. Tell him that you don't wanna be taking orders from a bitch and you would like to do your own thing. This should eventually make him show his hand and reveal who the other traitors are. You understand?"

"Yes, ma'am, I'm with you."

"Okay man, if you're really with me, stop calling me ma'am, okay? It makes me feel old although we're not that far apart in age," she said smiling.

"Okay, I understand," he said, smiling sheepishly. "But Mrs. Stallworth, I have a request."

"And what's that, Macky Boy?"

"When the time comes, will you grant me the honors of kill-ing this muthafucka myself?" Sugar sipped her Hen.

"Macky Boy, I can assure you that when that time comes, that muthafucka is all yours."

Chapter 28

Sugar's First Test
(Bitch better have my money)

One week later, after Tony's probable cause hearing which got postponed on the state's request, the word on the street was that Tony was finished, which made it a trying and dangerous time for Sugar. When a cat got knocked off on a dope charge or any other case that carried significant time, and it appeared that he wouldn't be hitting the turf anytime soon, it never failed. The niggas who were delinquent on their bread, would either hold out to the end or outright buck altogether on their debts. And there were the few, who would even talk shit because they knew, or at least figured, the person wouldn't be coming back in the near future to check that shit. Case in point: Chino Parsons. One evening Sugar received a call from the Professor complaining about Chino, who was head of the west coast operations. Sugar listened intently as the Professor ran down the Chino situation.

"Hey Sugar, sorry to bother with you with this, but this cat Chino on the west coast been holding out on Tony's bread ever since he's been down. On top of that, I heard from associates out west that he's also been talking big shit that Tony's finished and that he wasn't going to work for no...."

"Work for no, bitch?" Sugar finished.

"Yeah, that's exactly what he said. I just didn't wanna repeat it."

"Well, I will tell you like this, Professor. Mr. Chino is right about one thing. I am in fact a bitch, but that's the *only* thing he's right about."

"Okay, well what do you want done to the nigga?"

"I tell you what, Professor. Let me have a heart to heart talk chat with Mr. Chino to get a better understanding on where he's coming from first, and maybe he will get his mind right."

"Alright, Sugar. But let me know what you want me to do about the situation if nothing changes." After hanging up, Sugar sat at her study desk with a slight smirk on her face as she sipped on her Hen while the song *Bitch Better Have My Money* by Rihanna played in the background. A minute later she placed a call to Chino. After about six rings someone picked up.

"Yeah! Who is it?" he said rudely into the speakerphone.

"Is this Chino?"

"Yeah this Chino! Who wants to know?"

"Now, Mr Chino, is that anyway for you to answer the phone? Your mamma didn't teach you better manners than that?"

"Who the fuck is this?"

"This is Tony's woman, Sugar, from collections. And you're delinquent on your payments." Chino paused momentarily.

"Ohhhh! Mrs. Stallworth! I didn't know this was you," he said, snapping his fingers and motioning for his girl and entourage to be quiet.

"Sure you didn't know it was me, Chino, because we've never met."

"No, ma'am, unfortunately we haven't. By the way, how's Tony doing?" She totally ignored his question.

"Well, being that we haven't made formal introductions, I'm Sugar, but it's Mrs. Stallworth to you. The bitch you work for, the bitch you owe and the bitch you need to be getting at in the next uhhh....twenty-four hours." Chino frowned and gritted his teeth.

"I don't owe you shit, bitch! I owe Tony! But since he's looking to take the long ride, I think I'll just hold on to this bread for *the next twenty-five years to life!*" he said before letting out a wicked laugh that echoed throughout the house.

Sugar sipped on her Hen smiling and responded in a calm, but ominous tone.

"Okay, Mr. Chino. I see. Is that your final position on this? If so, I really do think you may wanna reconsider that, because this could be a big turning point or one of those life changing events, you know?" Chino paused to think about it for a few seconds after sensing not only the calmness in her voice, but also the deadly serious tone of it. However, his greed and ego took center stage.

"Like I said, bitch, I don't owe you shit! And don't call me no goddamn more either!" Still calm and sipping her Hen, she smiled.

"Okay, Mr. Chino, you've made your choice. And you know what they say about life. It really is about choices. Have a nice evening, Chino," she said, as she resumed sipping on her drink.

Chino hung up his cell, and immediately began weighing the consequences of his actions in his mind. The whole room was eerily silent after everyone heard the exchange. Like Chino, perhaps they pondered what was to come next. His whole crew, including his girlfriend, stood frozen peering at him with their eyes stretched wide as he looked over at them trying to appear confident and unafraid.

"That bitch must be crazy or high as hell if she think she can just muscle me into paying her!" he said laughing.

"Chino, baby, maybe you need to go ahead and pay that woman. She sounded pretty serious," his girl said. One of his men agreed.

"Yeah, Chino, man. You heard about what they did to that O.G. cat Natty Boy? One of my cousins who live there in Brooklyn told me they wiped out his entire organization and his affiliates, saved him for last then took him to the zoo and fed his ass to the polar bears."

"Yeah and he was alive and conscious when they ate him," someone else added. A collective grimace settled on the faces of all those present, including Chino's. He stared off in space momentarily seemingly trying to visualize the gruesome picture. But he quickly snapped back in a show of arrogance and defiance.

"Well, I ain't no muthafuckin' Natty Boy! And that was Tony who offed the nigga, not his bitch! She can't be as ruthless as him!" Chino then turned to his girl and grabbed her by the throat. "And bitch, the next time you talk outta turn, I'm gonna kick you out on your funky ass and send you back to the muthafuckin' corner where I found you sellin' pussy! You hear me, bitch!"

"Yes!" she screeched. Her eyes immediately turned bloodshot red and bulged out of her head. Chino then slung her down on the couch.

"*Now, is there anymore bitches in here?*" All of his men remained silent as his girl staggered into the bathroom to analyze herself in the mirror.

"That bitch ain't gonna do shit to Chino!" he said, brandishing his pistol in the air. "If she do try some shit, we'll be ready for her bitch ass! So y'all niggas stop worrying! Ole cowards!" he said laughing.

Later that night, a little after the clock struck midnight, a hit squad was dispatched to Chino's crib. There were a total of ten killers to make sure Chino didn't live to see the next day. After quickly taking out his six Rottweilers with silencers, the hit team scaled his two-story crib using ropes and ladders. Once they got to the top balcony, they all slipped in one by one as Chino and his men sat around the table playing dominoes, smoking weed, snorting lines of coke and listening to the loud music blaring from the component stereo speakers. The song, *Here I Go* by the Godfather played on while the hit team began scouring the interior of the house.

Gangsta Shyt

Chino's girl was lying across the bed still sobbing when she caught a glimpse of the killers crouched low clutching their pistols when one of them put his finger to his mouth and said, "Shhh!" She complied as they continued to creep on toward their target who was totally unaware of what was coming. When the hit team slipped into the room catching Chino's men off guard, they all froze as their boss snorted a line of Coke into his nose like a Kirby vacuum cleaner, while he steadily talked shit.

"Yeah that bitch got some fuckin' nerve telling Chino what to muthafuckin' do! Shiiid! Fuck the bitch and Tony!" he said as the hit team just stood there watching this fool and not saying a word. Chino had no idea as to the presence of these masked gunmen standing right there in the same room with him, because he was too busy with his head down in the plate of coke.

"Damn!" he said with his head down in the plate. "Why y'all niggas so quiet?" When they didn't answer he looked around and saw why. "*Oh shit!*" he said with coke falling from his nostrils. "Who the fuck is y'all and how did y'all get in here?"

The lead masked gunman walked up to him and said, "Now who the fuck do you think we are, silly nigga? That bitch you said you wasn't going to pay sent us here to see you!" A coked up Chino had a confused look on his face as though he was trying to figure out who and what the hell he was talking about. The gunman then picked up the phone and placed a call to Sugar.

"Hello, Mrs. Stallworth? I've got someone standing next to me who would like to have a word with you." As the killer pushed the phone towards him, Chino shook his head not wanting to talk. Knowing he didn't have much of a choice in the matter, he took the phone and said with a sheepish look on his face, "Hello."

"Mr. Chino! How is your night going so far?" Sugar said, smiling. Chino developed a lump in his throat.

"Not too good right now," he said, looking at the team of killers posted up around the room. "But...but...Mrs. Stallworth. I wanna apologize about earlier."

"So I can see you've found some manners now," she said. "Very good, Mr. Chino, very good. Now do me a favor and put that man standing next to you with that gun in his hand, back on the phone, would you please, sir?" A petrified and scared shitless Chino did exactly as she said and handed him the phone.

"Yes, Mrs. Stallworth?"

"Go ahead and let Mr. Chino know how much of a bitch I really am."

"Okay, ma'am, roger that," the gunman said before he laid the phone down. He then turned to Chino. "Hey nigga, Mrs. Stallworth sends her regards," he said before squeezing off a shot hitting Chino in the chest, causing him to collapse to the floor. The rest of the killers all walked by in a single file line shooting Chino at least three times a piece as they passed by him. His lifeless body lifted off the floor with every shot. Chino's men stood frozen as they looked on in horror and thinking they would be next. After the deed was done, the gunman spoke into the phone.

"Okay, Mrs. Stallworth, we gave Mr. Chino your regards. Is there anything else?"

"Yeah, there is one more thing. Put his lieutenant on the phone."

"Hey, which one of y'all is this nigga's lieutenant?"

A tall lanky cat with an afro bravely stepped forward and said with a little base in his voice, "I am."

The killer smiled then handed him the phone.

"Hello."

"Who am I speaking to?" Sugar asked.

"I'm T.C.," he said.

"Okay, T.C. I gotta question for you. Are you scared right now?"

"Yes ma'am. Very much so," he answered, looking over at the killers.

"Well good. Now I don't have to worry about you fuckin' with my money. You're now in charge of the west coast operations. Can you handle that, T.C.?"

"Yes ma'am," he said with a look of relief on his face. "I can handle it."

"Perfect, T.C. You take care and we'll be in touch," Sugar said before hanging up the phone and retiring for the evening. One by one hit the team exited the house and disappeared into the night. In her first real test of leadership, Sugar passed with flying colors, thus gaining the respect and admiration of not only Tony's organization, but everyone else on the street who heard about this incident. This test of leadership which represented a potentially make or break situation, proved one more thing about the new head of Tony's organization - she was just as ruthless and resolute as her old man, and just like him, she was not the one to fuck with.

Over the next several weeks, Sugar visited Tony every day while his empire ran more efficiently than ever, with distribution expanding to three more states. Under Sugar's command, Tony's organization was now moving over six thousand bricks a month, forcing Armando to enlist the help of another supplier in Columbia in order to keep up with demand. This was one of the largest cocaine distribution networks in the country, making Sugar the new undisputed Queen of the cocaine trade. Her reach was long, her power absolute, and she ruled with an iron fist. No one dared to openly challenge her, but she knew there were those, like the Professor, who were busy secretly plotting behind the scenes to undermine and destroy Tony and hijack his organization, and little did she know the plot had come full circle.

CATO

Chapter 29

The Professor Makes His Move

On Saturdays Rikers Island rec yard was always packed and bustling with activity with a diverse group of inmates splintered off into various gang and racial factions. The main centers of all activity were on the weight pile, common areas, and basketball courts where those groups congregated, plotted, and hustled, and where the occasional stabbings or gang fights took place. This is exactly why the sniper hack in the gun towers looked on with a wary eye and itchy trigger finger, and perhaps hoping and praying for some shit to pop off.

Even behind bars, Tony and Genie were feared and respected. Anywhere they went on the compound, there were always four to five soldiers accompanying them at all times, along with certain guards on the payroll, to guarantee their temporary stay at Rikers was as smooth and comfortable as possible.

"Genie, I have a strong feeling that the Professor will make his move any day now," Tony said, as they strolled the yard flanked by the soldiers.

"Well, whenever he do, T, we'll be ready for him."

"I'm not worried about us, Genie. I'm worried about my woman." Genie smiled and shook his head.

"T, man, hasn't it occurred to you by now that Sugar is more than capable of taking care of herself? Damn, bruh! She's a fuckin' boss now! With people like her, shit like that just comes natural."

"Yeah, I know, Genie. But regardless of all that, a man is still going to worry about his woman."

"Yeah, I feel you, bruh."

Suddenly their conversation was interrupted their by an announcement from the loudspeakers. "Antonio Stallworth to visitation! Antonio Stallworth to visitation!

"Speaking of the boss!" Tony said, smiling. "My baby is here to see me."

"Yeah, we done talked her up," Genie said, chuckling. "Like I said, my brother, with a broad like Sugar, you have absolutely nothing to worry about, man." Tony smiled and looked at his watch.

"Yeah and she's a little early too. Guess she missed me."

"Hey you two go with him," Genie said to the soldiers.

"Nah, Genie, let'em catch a break. I'm good. I'll holla at you later," Tony said before taking off to visitation. As Genie watched his partner rush off to see his old lady, he smiled and thought to himself, *Those two are made for each other. I wish I had a woman like Sugar. Let me stop telling that damn lie. I wish I had seven like her, one for each day of the week.* But almost as soon as he said that, something clicked in his mind. His instincts told him that something wasn't quite right. Sugar never came this early in the morning. He motioned to the soldiers.

"Hey man, y'all come with me!" he said before they hurried off to catch up with Tony. They were careful not to run as not to attract the attention of the killers in the towers who had their high powered rifles trained on the yard. After clearing the first flight of stairs, Tony headed through the long corridor leading to the visitation room. When he got to the end of the hallway two inmates jumped from behind the corner. One of them lunged with a shank, but Tony quickly sidestepped him at the last second.

"Nigga, you fixing to die!" one of the assailants said, as Tony immediately jumped into a defensive position. The second cat moved in quickly and took a swing at him with a metal pipe, but Tony ducked and hit him with a two punch combination to the body and jaw that dropped him to the pavement. Bouncing on his

feet in rhythm, Tony turned to face the other nigga who had begun taking short jabs at him with the shank. When he finally
caught Tony in the shoulder, Tony shot him a beautiful two piece
to the chin followed by a straight right that crumbled him to the
floor. Tony then backed up and grabbed his shoulder as the pain
finally reached the nerve center of his brain. The blood streamed
from between his fingers. Just as both assailants made it back to
their feet and shook off the blow to their domes that made them
temporarily groggy, they began closing in on Tony and cornering
him. When Tony's back made contact with the wall, and the men
blocked any escape routes, Genie and the soldiers rushed around
the corner and began inflicting murder on them, killing one instantly.

"You okay, T?" Genie asked, running up to him.

"Yeah, I'm good, bruh. The nigga just nicked me a little." he
said, holding his wounded shoulder. Genie then turned and
looked over at the surviving assailant the soldiers had completely
subdued.

"Bring him over here behind the staircase!" he said to the soldiers. The soldiers compiled and dragged him by his neck over to
where Genie was standing. "Alright nigga who sent you?" Genie
asked, while one of the soldiers forced the assailant to face him,
but he remained silent with a show of defiance on his face. Genie
frowned. "Look muthafucka! I'm gonna ask you one more goddamn time and if you don't tell me what I wanna know, not only
am I gonna kill you, I'm gonna find out who your family is and
murder them muthafuckas too! Now who sent you, nigga?"

"A cat named the Professor, man," he said in a defeated
voice. Genie looked over at Tony before motioning to the soldiers. As he and Tony walked away from the scene, the assailant
screamed like a bitch as the soldiers pushed the shank deep into
his heart. Genie analyzed Tony's shoulder wound.

"T, I'm thinking it will take about one or two stitches to close this gash. Luckily, the shank was dull." After Genie summoned for one of the guards they had on the payroll, they were able to slip Tony in the infirmary without logging him in. Not long after having his wound attended to, and changing out of the blood stained shirt, Tony got a visit from Sugar, but this time it was for real.

"Hey baby!" Sugar said with the usual wide smile on her face.

"Hello, babygirl," he said with a slight grimace on his face. Noticing something was wrong, Sugar asked, "Are you okay, Tony? You look like you're in pain or something."

"Yeah, babygirl, I'm okay. I got nicked a little in the shoulder earlier by a couple of cats, but I'm okay."

"*What!* Someone tried to harm you?"

"Yeah, baby, but really, I'm okay. I'm just a little sore."

"Are you sure you okay, baby?"

"Yeah, babygirl. I took some pain meds, so I'll be okay."

"It was that fuckin' Professor, wasn't it?" she said as an almost uncontrollable rage invaded her heart. Her body tensed up and her eyes nearly turned bloodshot red almost immediately. How *dare* this nigga fuck with her dude! He just crossed the line.

"Yeah, babygirl, it was him. One of those cats told us that he was the one who commissioned them. But listen, Sugar! Don't do anything yet!"

"And why not, Tony?"

"Because, babygirl, we need to know for sure who the other traitors are first before we make any move, you dig?"

"Yeah okay, Tony, I dig, but how long will we let this nigga get away with this shit? He's getting bolder and bolder with each move!"

"*Look baby!* We can't do nothing right now! I know what I'm doing, okay?" The bark of his alpha male voice seemed to humble her down. Besides, she knew he was right.

218

"Okay, I understand. I already got Macky Boy on trying to find out who the others are. But listen. As soon as he find out everything we need to know, I swear on my grandmamma, I'll handle it, baby."

"Okay, babygirl, but just use your head and not your emotion. In the meantime, be careful because I believe he'll try and hit you next since he missed me." She thought to herself.

Yeah and I'll be waiting on that muthafucka too.

"Okay, babygirl, these meds are really starting to kick in something serious. I can barely stay up. So I think I'll go back and lay down and get some rest."

"Okay, Tony baby, but are you sure you're alright, baby?" she said monitoring him carefully.

"Yeah, babygirl, I'm sure," he said before standing up. "But remember all that I said and stay vigilant."

"I will, Tony. Don't worry. You just get some rest. I love you."

"Love you too, babygirl," he said, blowing her a kiss before exiting the booth. Angry and pissed, Sugar rushed from the building, followed by her bodyguards, and stopped at a pay phone to place a call to Macky Boy.

"Hey look! Those muthafuckas tried to kill Tony today!"

"What!" he said.

"Yeah, so what do you have for me, because this shit has went on long enough!" Sugar was at her wits end with this Professor business. She had to constantly keep reminding herself that she could not allow her emotions to get the best of her and make a fucked up move that would jeopardize everything and put Tony in further peril. But how much more of this fuckery could a boss bitch take without exploding and having everyone killed? That would be much easier than exercising a patience that she never really had, unlike her old man who had the patience of an ambush predator. However, she was under strict orders to stand down and lie in wait.

"Mrs. Stallworth, I found out everything! From who's down with the Professor to what they're plotting now."

"Okay, Macky Boy, I don't wanna discuss this on a pay phone, so meet me at Junior's on Dekalb and Flatbush in two hours."

"I'll be there, Mrs. Stallworth."

Exactly two hours later, Macky Boy walked into Junior's to see Sugar sitting at a table in the far back of the restaurant. As soon as he sat down, he began running down to her detail by detail on the Professor's plan to waste her and take the next shipment. Now Sugar had what she needed. She had the green light to make her next move on the traitors in the organization. Sandman, G, Chi-town, Lil' Larry, Black, and the Professor who was the lead conspirator, were all going to be in for the shock of their lives at the next organizational meeting, which always fell on the day of the monthly shipments, and this time coincidentally on Tony's birthday.

Before walking out, Sugar looked at Macky Boy and said, "Okay, Macky Boy, you be ready, for on that day, I'm going to clean up my man's organization on the day he was born into this world. And I can promise you, it will be a birthday present that his enemies will never forget."

Chapter 30

Wrong House, Wrong Bitch

The morning before the meeting and Tony's birthday, Sugar visited him, and this time Genie was allowed to visit with them, after Tony pulled some strings.

"Hey, babygirl, look who the hacks let me drag down here," Tony said smiling, and pointing at Genie. Sugar laughed.

"Hey, Genie Boy! How are you?!"

"I'm good, Sugar. Just trying to keep this man of yours here in one piece."

"Well, you better do just that, Genie, or you will have to answer to his woman." They all laughed out loud. While they reminisced about recent and old times, Sugar also filled them in on the details concerning the Professor's treachery. Toward the end of the visit, Tony informed her that since the state had no eyewitnesses and no evidence, they had only twenty days left to file formal charges or cut them loose. This was obviously some welcomed news for Sugar who was ready for the return of her King.

After saying her goodbyes to Tony and Genie, she went to the crib to wind down and prepare for tomorrow's much anticipated meeting. Shortly after briefing her security to remain on high alert, she placed a call to her grandmother and talked with her for nearly an hour. Afterwards, she lit some candles and ran a steaming hot bubble bath before turning on some music and fixing a double shot of Hen. After returning to the bathroom and closing the door behind her, she slipped out of her clothes and slid down in the hot relaxing bubble bath.

Lying there in a relaxed state and in near complete darkness if it were not for the flickering flame of the burning candle, Sugar took short sips of her drink as the old school song *The Look of Love* by Isaac Hayes, echoed through the huge mansion. She was totally unaware of the events transpiring outside. The video monitors in the bedrooms and living room showed two shadowy figures in all black attire creeping up and ambushing her four bodyguards by taking them out with silencers and with expert precision. The bodyguards never saw what hit'em. The two masked killers then began to gain access into the mansion using burglar's tools. While they continued on trying to disarm the alarm, Sugar continued to relax, still totally oblivious to what was coming her way. After a few more minutes of painstaking effort, the killers finally struck pay dirt and disarmed the mansion's security system.

Once inside, they immediately began searching for their target, methodically going from room to room, clutching their pistol equipped silencers as the music continued to echo through the crib. The two killers, identical twin albino brothers who went by the name of the Shadow Twins out of Harlem, who were equally identical cold blooded killers, scoured the crib for their prey like a duo of Velociraptors. The manner in which they moved smoothly and effortlessly through the home, lock step, in sync and in rhythm, indicated that they were a team who had done this together many times before.

Legend had it that they once breached a heavily guarded site of a meeting between competing syndicate groups, and by the time the twins exited the premises, no one inside came out alive, with the exception of a waitress who hid behind the bar when their silencers started speaking their deadly whispers. When the police arrived on the scene, they found bodies inside and out with no physical evidence left behind, with the exception of two bullets left standing upright side by side on the bar which was the twin's calling cards that almost every hitter left behind to let the relevant parties signifying that this was their work.

After scouring the entire mansion, the two killers zeroed in on the bathroom where Sugar was. Figuring she was inside, they just stood there at the door listening for any movements, but the loud music made it virtually impossible to hear anything. Unable to make out whether anyone was inside, one of the twins gently twisted the doorknob to find it unlocked. With a sadistic grin on his face, perhaps delighted at the prospect of another kill, the killer slowly eased the door open as Sugar continued to lay there in the bathtub not moving, and not making a sound while the song *The Hills* by The Weekend echoed off the mansion's walls from the surround sound's speakers, as the two killers closed in on her.

Once they finally made it to the bathtub, which sat about fifty feet from the door, one of them cautiously clutched the shower curtain then motioned to the other to get ready to fire. Holding three fingers in the air, he gave the sign for his partner to fire on the count of three. With his closed fist in the air he counted, one, two, three, then suddenly snatched the shower curtain open, and the very next thing he saw and heard were bright orange explosions from the nickle plated .38 snub nose in Sugar's hand. The dark bathroom lit up with each pull of the trigger. The first shot hit the lead assassin in his chest, putting him square on his back. The second, third, and fourth shots hit his twin brother, flipping him up against the bathroom door, leaving him immobile and unable to move a muscle. The hollow points had ripped through his chest and mushroomed out of his back, severing his spinal cord. As they both laid there sprawled on the bathroom floor moaning and writhing in pain, Sugar stood up in the bathtub with the smoking pistol in her hand, and soap suds oozing down her naked body.

"Now what the fuck y'all doing in Sugar's house?" she asked, stepping out of the bathtub and making her way over to them, but the two men didn't answer. They just continued to whine and moan in agony while Sugar stood straddled over them. They were carrying on so loudly, they actually drowned out the music. Standing there with a menacing cold blooded smile, and taking careful aim with the snub nose held tightly in her hand, Sugar said, "Wrong house, wrong bitch!" then fired point blank range into the two brothers, bringing their suffering and their assassin days to an abrupt and tragic end.

The impact from the .38 hollow points lifted their bodies off the floor with each shot. The last thing they saw other than the bright orange fire that came from the barrel of Sugar's pistol, was her well-groomed, well-shaved cat as she stood over them. Much to their detriment, the killers made one fatal mistake when they disabled the mansion's alarms. They didn't take into consideration there was a back-up alarm on the bathroom wall over the bathtub which had a red light that flickered whenever there was any movement in the interior of the house. To Tony's credit and acute security mindedness, he installed it when he purchased the home.

Chapter 31

Settling All Bets

Early the next morning, Sugar met up with Macky Boy and briefed him on the game plan. He in turn briefed his crew of killers he brought from his hood in Yonkers who were brought in especially for this event. The most important aspect of this plan was the element of surprise when Sugar showed up as big as day right there in front of the Professor and the other traitors.

Ten minutes before the meeting was set to start, one by one the members started filing into the conference room as the Professor stood at the door smiling and greeting them. After the last member walked in, followed by Macky Boy, the Professor looked at his watch supremely confident that Sugar was a no show due to her recent untimely assassination. At three minutes till, the Professor began the meeting.

"Okay, gentleman, as I'm sure most of you know there's been another change in the organization. This change is part of a new direction and a new way of doing things, but with me as the new...."

"Sho' you right!" Sugar interrupted and said as she walked in the conference room smiling, causing everyone to turn around in their seats. The Professor and the other traitors looked as if they had just seen a ghost. "Am I late?" she asked the Professor. Before he could find the words to respond, "Nope!" she said looking at her diamond watch. "It's exactly ten sharp. In addition to a few other skills I learned from Tony, punctuality is the one I really had to work on." she said, smiling.

"Hey Sugar," the Professor said sheepishly. "I took it upon myself to start the meeting, figuring you would be late."

"And why would you think I'd be late, Professor? Have I ever been late to a meeting before? Better yet, why would you start without me when I'm the one who calls and moderates all the meetings?"

"Well, uhhh I thought..."

"Well, you thought wrong, Professor," she said, cutting him off. "Now have a seat."

"Okay, Sugar, my apologies," he said as he took his seat at the round table alongside the rest of the members. The sweat was beginning to appear on his forehead, as well as the others.

"Apology accepted," she said before addressing the members. "First of all gentlemen, I wanna start by reiterating what the Professor said about this organization heading in a new direction. In fact, after today, there's going to be some slight changes in the structure of this organization. But before we get to that, I wanna to say to everyone, through your hard work and dedication, we are bigger than ever. In fact, because of that hard work and dedication, we have expanded our distribution to a total of ten states, and I'm confident we will eventually double that number within a year or two. With you gentlemen, nothing is impossible in terms of the business we're in. With you gentlemen, we can go global."

Everyone began to applaud, including the Professor and the others who at the beginning of the meeting had begun to sweat bullets, but now they all had a sense of relief on their faces, which was exactly Sugar's intent. Her plan all along was to lure them all into a false sense of security. "There are other markets that have caught my interest - markets over in Europe which at the present time I strongly believe will generate more profits, which will of course increase prosperity for everyone. This is what Tony created and established for you all so everyone could eat and live well."

Just as the applause began again, she raised her hand in the air to silence them. "But unfortunately, there are some of you who don't have a genuine appreciation for this thing my man created." At this point, everyone began looking around at each other with suspicion as the nervous tension returned to the room. A nervous tension that was so thick, it could be cut with a knife. "Now I'm not going to name names or any shit like that at this time, but you know who you are, and if you wanna remain a part of this organization you had better make some attitude adjustments and get your minds right."

The Professor and his co-conspirators' guilt was so evident, they made a pathetic attempt to hide it, but couldn't. Macky Boy cracked a slight grin because he knew they were all just about ready to shit on themselves.

"Okay now. For that other order of business," she said before motioning her head to one of the soldier's standing at the entrance way. He then left the room momentarily, at which point the room became so quiet a rat pissing on cotton could be heard. Sugar continued to stand there patiently at the podium twiddling her thumbs awaiting his return, while the room remained eerily silence. Seconds later, the soldier returned with a silver platter with a dome lid covering it, placed it down in the middle of the round table before posting up back at the door. Every single member's eyes were trained on the silver platter, curious as to its contents. The silence in the room was akin to a wake, but minus the wailing and soft music.

As Sugar scanned the room, she seemed to take a somewhat sadistic satisfaction in seeing the guilty among them sweat. Pacing back and forth on her high heeled boots in front of the podium, with her hands in her pockets, she began to speak again. "You know, someone once said if you don't have anyone or anything in this world you would die or kill for, this life just isn't worth living. As for me, there's only one person, with the exception of my grandmother that I love more than anything in this world, and that's my man, Tony. Pausing for a second, she looked around the room before continuing. "Tony means everything to me. And there is *nothing,* I mean *no-thing* I wouldn't do for him.

So what makes anyone in their right muthafuckin' mind think that I would allow *one hair* on his lovely head to be harmed or fucked with in any way?" she said with her voice rising. Her eyes displayed a deadly serious finality in them that said *this is it*. Everyone, including the Professor, sat there with a frozen, petrified look on their faces. She continued.

"Last night, I nearly died for my man, but today, I will *kill* for my man." Immediately after she said that, a team of soldiers rushed in and started murdering everyone involved with the Professor while the innocent party looked on in sheer terror. Some were shot point blank range in their domes multiple times with pistols equipped with silencers, and the other less fortunate ones were garroted with piano wire, dying a slow, painful, agonizing death. Sandman, G, Chi-town, Black, Lil' Larry, and Tripp were all wasted right there at the round table where they sat. Some of them laid face down on the table, in their plates of refreshments, in a pool of blood. Others lay back in their chairs lifeless with their eyes and mouths wide open in shock. The Professor had attempted to run, but Macky Boy put his Glock to his temple and made him sit his ass back down at the table. After the vicious bloodletting had ended, the soldiers then dragged the dead member's bloody corpses away.

Sugar then walked over to the silver platter and removed the lid, revealing two severed heads belonging to the Shadow Twins who were sent to waste her at her crib the night before. The remaining members all let out a collective gasp at the gruesome display in front of them.

"Do these faces look familiar to you, Professor?" she asked smiling. The Professor did not answer. He just sat there totally speechless with a look of terror on his face. He knew at this point, it was game over. "Since the Professor is all lost for words right now, I'll answer that question for him. These heads here used to belong to the two gentlemen the Professor commissioned and sent to my crib last night as part of his new direction, which was to assassinate me and Tony, then take the next shipment." Just as the Professor was about to plead his case, Sugar put her finger to her lips and shushed him every time he attempted to speak. She continued.

"So not only did he attempt to have us wasted, he also dropped a dime on Tony and Genie just so he could take over this organization." Hearing this, all of the members cut their eyes at him and looked at him with utter contempt. "And this was his new direction. But the one thing he didn't count on, the one person he underestimated and never factored into the equation, was me, Tony's bitch!"

With that said, she snapped her fingers and Macky Boy immediately put two shots in the back of the Professor's head. His limp body dropped to the floor and began kicking and wiggling in involuntary movements. One of the soldiers stepped forward, grabbed him by his feet and dragged him away, leaving a trail of blood, brain matter, and skull fragments smeared on the linoleum. Sugar then walked back to the podium and stared at everyone with an icy cold look on her face before asking, "Soooooo, are there any questions, comments, statements or objections to anything that uhhh, happened here today?"

No one said a word or so much as moved a muscle or changed the expression on their faces. They knew not to. Sugar then smiled and clasped her hands together.

"Well good! Now we're all one big happy family again, just as Tony had envisioned it. He would be proud," she said as everyone let out a collective sigh of relief, realizing that the nightmare situation in the conference room was now over. "Speaking of Tony," she said, "he and Genie will be out in twenty days, so he can assume his rightful place as the head of this organization he founded," she said as the members all stood up and gave a standing ovation. "I would also like to take this time to announce that Macky Boy is the new Capo." This brought another round of applauds as all the members looked over at the youngster. "If there's nothing else gentlemen, before I adjourn this meeting I wanna leave you all with something. This organization my man put together is as sweet as sugar, and don't you ever forget it," she said before walking away from the podium and exiting the conference room, followed by her soldiers amid the applause.

In what was truly a crisis situation, Sugar stood up in the pain and reached deep down inside of herself to transform into something that she never imagined becoming, which was, one ruthless boss bitch at the reigns of a multi-million dollar criminal enterprise. But she did what she had to do without question, without inquiry, or even without a moment's hesitation, and it was all done for her man, Antonio *Tony* Stallworth.

Chapter 32

Hey Love

Dressed in a white Chinchilla fur coat and hat with dark shades on, Sugar stood waiting beside the black Bentley as the cool northern winds gently blew off the water's surface. The soldiers, in trench coats and dark shades, stood guard on the docks with a wary eye scanning the horizon as their boss lady stared at the East River anxiously awaiting for her proverbial ship to come in. In this case, it was the prison ferry that would return her old man back into her life. Though it seemed like an eternity, it had been only six months since he was hauled away for what she had feared at the time would be forever, never to be in her arms again. But it was once said by a wise man, "As long as there's life, there's hope." And from day one, Sugar represented both his life and his hope.

Now it was time for their lives to pick up and resume where it had left off before the brief interruption. But this time, with a new perspective and hopefully with a whole new scope and purpose. The life that Tony had provided for them, though fantastic, was by no means a permanent way of life, and he gave her his word that it wouldn't be in exchange for her assuming the reigns of his empire in his absence. And he had every intention on making good on his word. However, there's also another old saying by an unknown author: *Promises are made to be broken.*

As the ferry carrying her man crept ever closer inland, his curly hair came into full view, producing a smile on Sugar's face. As Sugar came into his full view, a smile began to emerge on his own face as he recognized the beautiful lady standing next to the Bentley amongst the other people waiting impatiently for the return of their loved ones who were returning from captivity.

Now in full view, enough to see the whites of one another's eyes, the old school joint *Hey Love* by the Delfonics blared appropriately from the Bentley's speakers. When the ferry finally made contact with the dock, and the freed captives all scattered in their own directions to reunite with their families, Tony moved towards his woman with his eyes locked on hers, walking in a straight line as if he was in a trance. Once they embraced, they kissed and held each other tightly as if they were the only inhabitants left on planet earth, with no worries, and no other focus on anything else but each other. As the people all cleared out, leaving Tony and Sugar there alone, with the exception of the soldiers, they stood there in silence, in one spot for the next twenty minutes in each other's arms.

The END OF THIS ORDEAL, BUT NOT END OF STORY.

To Be Continued...
Coming Soon
Gangsta Shyt 2

Gangsta Shyt

<u>Coming Soon From Lock Down Publications</u>

RESTRAINING ORDER

By **CA$H & Coffee**

NO LOYALTY NO LOVE

By **CA$H & Reds Johnson**

GANGSTA SHYT **II**

By **CATO**

PUSH IT TO THE LIMIT

By **Bre' Hayes**

GANGSTA CITY **II**

By **Teddy Duke**

BLOOD OF A BOSS **III**

By **Askari**

SHE DON'T DESERVE THE DICK

SILVER PLATTER HOE **III**

By **Reds Johnson**

BROOKLYN ON LOCK **III**

By **Sonovia Alexander**

THE STREETS BLEED MURDER **III**

By **Jerry Jackson**

CONFESSIONS OF A DOPEMAN'S DAUGHTER **III**

By **Rasstrina**

NEVER LOVE AGAIN **II**

CATO

WHAT ABOUT US **III**

By **Kim Kaye**

A GANGSTER'S REVENGE **IV**

By **Aryanna**

GIVE ME THE REASON **II**

By **Coco Amoure**

LAY IT DOWN **II**

By **Jamaica**

I LOVE YOU TO DEATH

By Destiny J

Available Now

LOVE KNOWS NO BOUNDARIES **I II & III**

By **Coffee**

SILVER PLATTER HOE **I & II**

HONEY DIPP **I & II**

CLOSED LEGS DON'T GET FED **I & II**

A BITCH NAMED KOCAINE

NEVER TRUST A RATCHET BITCH **I & II**

By **Reds Johnson**

A DANGEROUS LOVE **I, II, III, IV, V, VI, VII**

By **J Peach**

CUM FOR ME

An **LDP Erotica Collaboration**

Gangsta Shyt

A GANGSTER'S REVENGE **I & II**

By **Aryanna**

WHAT ABOUT US **I & II**

NEVER LOVE AGAIN

By **Kim Kaye**

THE KING CARTEL **I, II & III**

By **Frank Gresham**

BLOOD OF A BOSS **I & II**

By **Askari**

THE DEVIL WEARS TIMBS **I, II & III**

BURY ME A G **I II & III**

By **Tranay Adams**

THESE NIGGAS AIN'T LOYAL **I, II & III**

By **Nikki Tee**

THE STREETS BLEED MURDER **I & II**

By **Jerry Jackson**

DIRTY LICKS

By **Peter Mack**

THE ULTIMATE BETRAYAL

By **Phoenix**

BROOKLYN ON LOCK **I & II**

By **Sonovia Alexander**

DON'T FU#K WITH MY HEART **I & II**

By **Linnea**

BOSS'N UP **I & II**

By **Royal Nicole**

LOYALTY IS BLIND

By **Kenneth Chisholm**

I LOVE YOU TO DEATH

By Destiny J

<u>BOOKS BY LDP'S CEO, CA$H</u>

TRUST NO MAN

TRUST NO MAN 2

TRUST NO MAN 3

BONDED BY BLOOD

SHORTY GOT A THUG

A DIRTY SOUTH LOVE

THUGS CRY

THUGS CRY 2

TRUST NO BITCH

TRUST NO BITCH 2

TRUST NO BITCH 3

TIL MY CASKET DROPS

Coming Soon

TRUST NO BITCH (KIAM EYEZ' STORY)

THUGS CRY 3

BONDED BY BLOOD 2

RESTRANING ORDER

NO LOYALTY NO LOVE

CATO

Made in the USA
Columbia, SC
15 June 2023

18057587R00134